HOSED

PIPPA GRANT
LILI VALENTE

Copyright © 2018 Pippa Grant and Lili Valente

All rights reserved. This book or any portion thereof may not be reproduced or used in any manner whatsoever without the express written permission of the publisher except for the use of brief quotations in a book review.

This is a work of fiction. Names, characters, businesses, places, events and incidents are either the products of the author's imagination or used in a fictitious manner. Any resemblance to actual persons, living or dead, or actual events is purely coincidental.

Cover design by Lori Jackson Designs.

Photograph Eric Battershell Photography

Edited by Jessica Snyder

ABOUT THE BOOK

HOSED
A Firefighter / Neighbor / Virgin Nerd Romance

The world's sexiest firefighter is about to get a second chance with the virgin next door...

He's bossy, arrogant, and so ridiculously hot he should come with a warning label and a pair of flame retardant coveralls.

He's also the boy who broke my heart when we were in high school.

I want to move in next door to Ryan O'Dell the way I want to be the virgin gamer geek suddenly in charge of running my sister's sex toy factory. Too bad both are written in my stars.

Yeah, I'm the world's oldest virgin code-writing nerd.

And he's the world's hottest firefighter.

And even though he intimidates the heck out of me, I can't seem to control my libido when he's around.

Where is my dignity? My self-respect? My panties?

Seriously…. Have you seen them? Anyone?

Maybe they're hiding in his bedroom. With my heart.

Yeah, I know. I'm hosed.

So hosed.

Hosed is a steamy, fun romantic comedy between a firefighter and the virgin nerd next door, complete with a pet raccoon, scandalous gossip, and dildo football. (No, really.) This romance has no cheating or cliffhangers, and ends with a banging hot happily ever after.

ONE

Ryan O'Dell
(aka a small-town firefighter unaware that a dildo is about to change his life)

THERE'S nothing like a good lube fire your first morning back from vacation.

Or so I assume. This is actually a first for our station. Can't help but wonder if it'll be the last.

Hank lays on the horn and slows the engine at the main intersection in Happy Cat, Georgia. We can see the Sunshine Sex Toys factory three blocks and one left ahead. But with Maud and Gerald Hutchins standing in the center of the road—him six-two, two-fifty, with a gray comb-over flapping above a hastily written *Let It Burn* sign, her five-ten, a buck-twenty-five, her hair dyed blue and coming out of its ponytail while she tries to shove him out of the way—we're not setting any rapid response records.

But there's no visible smoke at the factory.

Good sign.

Hank gets around the Hutchinses, aided by Maud, who claws at Gerald's tickle spot to keep him from darting in front of the truck.

Thirty seconds later, we're careening into the parking lot of the converted tobacco warehouse behind the post office/taxidermy shop. A couple dozen employees huddle near the azaleas at the far end of the lot while alarms blare from the building. We're out of the engine and halfway to the front door, already in turnout gear, when a woman on a bike plows into our group.

Hank dives, Jojo yelps, and I snag a handlebar before I realize what I'm grabbing.

A dildo.

The bike has dildo handlebars.

The woman leaps off. She barely comes up to my breastbone, though the messy chestnut bun piled on her head gives her another two inches. "Thanks," she calls as she darts toward the door.

I hustle after her. "Ma'am, you have to stay out of the building."

"Are you kidding?" she shoots over her shoulder without so much as a glance my way. "If the factory burns down on my watch, I'm dead meat anyway."

"Ma'am—"

"It's okay! It's out!" A lanky guy in an ash-streaked lab coat and safety goggles rushes through the door. "I did it! The lube fire is contained!"

"Keep them outside," Jessie, our chief, mutters to me while she and the rest of the crew push around us and stomp into the building.

I shift to the left and extend my arms, blocking the

woman and the lab rat as they start after the team. "Back up, please."

"But the fire's out. I need to see what kind of damage—"

"Back. Up. Please."

The Don't Mess With The Big Serious Firefighter Voice usually works like a charm, but not with this one. She's bouncing like a bird, trying to get around me. She'd probably dive between my legs if I gave her half an opening.

And not *dive between my legs* in the good way.

"It was the lube," the lab rat is telling Bird Girl. "The mango-lime-liberation flavor Savannah wanted us to sweeten up a bit. One minute, I'm mixing everything just fine, and the next, *poof*! Lube fire."

"Has this ever happened before?" she asks.

"No, never. We should call—"

"We are *not* calling Savannah." Bird Girl lifts a hand. "We are going to go inside, assess the damage, and—"

"No, we're going to back away from the building," I interject. "Now."

They both look at me, and *whoa*.

Bird Girl's eyes. They're somewhere between a mocha cappuccino and milk chocolate, big and round behind her glasses. She's not wearing makeup, but she doesn't need any. A flash of déjà vu hits me, along with a sudden realization that I have no idea who this woman is, which is practically impossible in Happy Cat. Secrets and strangers are rare things in a town as small as ours.

Her cupid's bow lips part, her dark lashes lift as her eyes flare, and a sliver of a dimple flashes when she stutters, "You have *got* to be kidding me."

I snap back to reality with a frown. "I'm not. Until the building is clear—"

"It's clear, it's clear," the lab rat says with a hand flutter. "I told you. I put it out."

An explosion inside the building rattles the windows. Not enough to break the glass, but enough to put my pulse into hyperdrive.

The lab rat shrieks, covers his head, and dashes across the parking lot.

I grab Brown Eyes by an arm and haul her over the blacktop while my radio squawks with reports about the crew inside.

Everyone's checking in. No injuries, but we need to clear the building. Five minutes ago.

"Who's missing? Who's still inside?" I ask the woman. "Are all the employees accounted for?"

"I don't know." She shoots a ghost-faced look back at the factory.

"Where's Savannah?"

"Vacation."

Vacation. Not likely—I read the town's gossip-heavy InstaChat page, and I know as well as everyone else what happened with Savannah—but also not the most pressing matter. "Then who's in charge here?"

"Um…me?"

I freeze. "You're in charge?"

Her round cheeks are turning pink. "It's complicated."

"Who can tell me if the building is empty?" I ask, hurrying across the last stretch of asphalt.

"One of them?" She motions toward the other Sunshine Sex Toys employees huddled in the grass at the edge of the parking lot. "Maybe Olivia?"

"Oh, yes, me! I can help! I'd love to help!" The familiar blonde waves, making the silver bangles draping her arms clank.

Under normal circumstances, I'd wince at Olivia

Moonbeam's eager enthusiasm. Right now, a wince isn't strong enough. "You know who might still be in the building?" I ask her.

Her lips purse. They're painted Goddess Core Pink, which I know because she made an announcement about it being her *signature feminine-power color* at the fish fry two weeks ago. My brothers have been making jokes about their "goddess cores" on a group text ever since.

"Well, no, we don't do roll call," Olivia says. "We're all about working when the energy is right. Letting vitality move organically through the chakras to the heart center and *then* the hands, you know?"

Unfortunately, I do. Since Olivia moved to Happy Cat I've learned more about my chakras and my "energetic soul body" than I ever wanted to know.

"Ruthie May?" I call. I know the town gossip works here. No idea what her job is, but it doesn't matter. She'll know who came to work today, what they were wearing, and whether or not they're feeling regular or still bound up from last night's nacho dip.

The familiar grandmotherly busybody hustles out from the middle of the crowd, her usually cheerful face drawn and serious under her dyed-brown hair. "Everyone's out and accounted for, darlin'. Well, except Frank, but he was testing some product over at Widow MacIntosh's place last night and is late gettin' in. And Savannah, of course, who's run off on account of her mental breakdown. But I'm sure you saw that on InstaChat."

"She did *not* have a mental breakdown," Brown Eyes hisses.

Ruthie May's weathered forehead wrinkles sympathetically. "Honey, she had an entire truck of dicks-in-a-box delivered to Steve's parents' house, then posted a video on InstaChat of her playing Whack-a-Husband with a dildo. If that ain't a mental breakdown—"

"He was cheating on her with a *sheep*," someone else in the crowd offers. "He earned that dildo beating."

"She was entitled to it!" another pipes up. "Especially with the grief she got just for telling the truth!"

"Back to the matter at hand, please," Bird Girl squeaks in an attempt to shift focus. But good luck with that. People are going to be talking about Savannah Sunderwell's breakdown when our children's children are riding to school in self-driven cars. Aside from Savannah coming home to open a sex toy factory in the first place, the situation surrounding her divorce is the biggest scandal Happy Cat has seen in years. "How did the fire start?" she continues, "and how do we stop anything like this from happening again?"

"The lube shouldn't have been flammable," the lab rat says. "I did all the calculations myself. The solution shouldn't start smoking until at least three hundred fifty degrees. We were still at room temperature, and none of the ingredients are particularly volatile. Unless I grabbed the wrong bottle…"

"So there's no one else in the building?" I clarify with Ruthie May.

"As far as I know." She gnaws on her lower lip as her gaze shifts to the brown-eyed woman. "Savannah isn't back in town, is she, Cassie? You talk to her today?"

Cassie…Cassie *Sunderwell*? Savannah's sister?

Fuck me with a spoon. I should've seen the resemblance.

But she's so…grown up. And wearing a tight white tee shirt with a cartoon Viking whose horns hit right at her nipples.

Damn. It's a damn good thing I'm here for a fire, or I might be staring.

"Savannah's *on vacation*," Cassie repeats. "She's not in the building. She's not even in the country."

"She's totally gone," Olivia agrees with a toss of her long blond hair. "She cleaned out half her bedroom and had me grab her a wide variety of vibrators to take along on her soul journey. Variety is important when you're healing a heart chakra wound."

Cassie opens her mouth, then closes it. Her cheeks are turning the right shade of pink to highlight the freckles on her nose, and for a split second, I wonder how many of Savannah's products *she's* tried.

At that moment, the sheriff finally decides to pull into the parking lot.

About damned time.

"Stay here," I tell the group of employees.

Cassie, Olivia, and Ruthie May all ignore the order, skittering after me as I stride to meet the sheriff, who's taking his sweet time climbing out of his cruiser.

Just a lube fire and some explosions. No big deal. Not worth rushing to.

He scratches his belly and looks around. "What we got goin' on here, Ry?"

"The lube exploded," Olivia says.

"I wasn't inside the lab when it happened," Ruthie May adds. "But if you ask me, it was probably a bad reaction between the eco-rubber in the self-lubricating butt plug and the lime in the mango-lime lube."

The sheriff chews on the ends of his mustache and stares at her, then turns to Cassie. "Where's Savannah?"

"I've got this one!" Olivia chirps happily. "She..."

"She left me in charge while she's on vacation," Cassie interrupts. "And right now, my priority isn't shocking the sheriff, ladies. It's making sure the factory doesn't burn down. So back off, Ruthie May. Quiet down, Olivia. And, you—" She points at me with a glower that leaves no wiggle room for interpretation. I'm apparently persona non grata with Cassie Sunderwell. "Take your pretty face off to help keep the building in one piece and make sure my sister doesn't have a reason to kill me, okay?"

That's probably a good plan. If that lab explosion gets out of hand, we'll need every firefighter in a thirty-mile radius for backup.

If there's as much lube in that building as I suspect there is, the entire town could be at risk.

With one last glance at grown-up Cassie, with her skintight shirt and unexpectedly sexy glasses, I head into the building.

I do not look back, I do not think about what a shame it is that Cassie seems to hate me like ass sores, and I do not dwell too long on the fact that she called me pretty.

Or how much I liked it…

TWO

*From the texts of Cassie Sunderwell and
Savannah Sunderwell*

Cassie: Hey, Savannah. How are you? I hope you're resting, relaxing, and showering yourself with the self-care you need to heal. I love you so much.

Savannah: I love you, too, sissy. And I'm okay. Still sporting a crater where my heart used to be, but if I keep stuffing my face with scones and clotted cream, it will eventually be filled with dairy and carbs.
Maybe.
If not, I'll move on to haggis next week when I get to Scotland.

Cassie: You do know that haggis is basically offal stuffed into a cow's stomach, right?

Savannah: Ugh! No. That's disgusting.
But it also sounds filling. Then my heart crater could be full of offal and awful.

Cassie: Oh, pumpkin. I know it hurts, but someday you'll look back on all this and be so glad you had an amazing opportunity to see the world and to do something just for yourself, I promise. Probably someday very soon!

Savannah: *zombie emoji* *heart emoji* *skull and crossbones emoji*

Cassie: Okay. I'll keep my platitudes to myself while you're nursing your wounded zombie heart, but there is a matter we need to discuss. Something happened today. But before I tell you about it, I want to assure you that everything is fine, no one was hurt, and the factory did NOT burn down.
So really, this is a happy story! A great story!
Nothing to be upset about at all.

Savannah: Oh my God! Was Gordon playing with fire again? I was so nervous when we moved in next to the taxidermy shop, but everyone in town promised he hadn't lit anything up in years!

Cassie: No, it wasn't Gordon. He wasn't into work yet and he does seem to be reformed as far as I can tell. Though I have to confess I'm creeped out by his shop window. When did he start the stuffed squirrels in battle gear thing?

Savannah: A few years ago. He's making a killing on Etsy. Can't keep enough Mighty Squirrels in stock to meet the demand. People are way into taxidermied rodents dressed as soldiers, apparently.

Cassie: People are disturbing.

Savannah: Agreed, but I'm more disturbed by fire right now. Olivia didn't take me seriously when I said we were going to light people's sheets on fire, did she? I was sure she understood that was a metaphor.

Cassie: No. No sheets. The investigation is still ongoing, but we know it started with some lube in the lab. Neil thought he'd put it out, but it ignited again after he left the building, spread to a bin of self-lubricating butt plugs he'd planned to use in another experiment, and then there was a loud, but mostly harmless, explosion.

Savannah: WHAT?!

Cassie: Turns out coconut oil is more flammable than one might assume.

Savannah: OH MY GOD. That's it. I'm closing down the factory. It's a sign from the universe. Everything I touch turns to poop. My marriage, my business, my life, my heart.

Cassie: Your heart is not poop. Your life is not poop! Steve is poop. You are unicorn hair plaited in a beautiful braid, sprinkled with sugar and sunshine.

Savannah: Thank you, but I'm done kidding myself, Cass. I should have closed everything down before I left town.

Cassie: No! You have a great team here. Everything's fine, and it'll be running like a well-lubed machine and waiting for you when you're ready to come back.

Savannah: I'm not coming back. I'm going to eat my way through the United Kingdom. Then I'm going to sail to the Netherlands and smoke my way through every pot shop in Amsterdam. After that, I'll drink my way through France until my money runs out and I end up homeless on a beach in Italy selling seashell necklaces to survive and talking to myself because I won't understand anyone else. But since I don't speak Italian, I won't be able to communicate, make friends, or fall in love, and my heart will never be broken again. So homeless madness will end up being a fair trade.

Cassie: Stop it. You are not going to end up homeless. You are going to grieve, get back on your feet, and reclaim the helm of this wonderful company you've built.

Savannah: You hate the company.

Cassie: I do not, I'm just…shy around dildos.

Savannah: You shouldn't be. Dildos just want to make you feel good, Cass. Dildos are our friends, unlike dicks attached to actual real life men.

Cassie: I don't think dildos have life goals, but I see your point.

Savannah: Good. You should take a few home and see which one you like the best. Take them all. I'm shutting down.

Cassie: Say I do take all your dildos. For argument's sake, not because I want one, much less all of them. Then where would the rest of the world find safe, eco-friendly sex products that put a woman's pleasure first? You're revolutionary, Savannah. You can't let humanity down.

Savannah: I can't give humanity's nether regions third-degree burns, either. Or God forbid, blow them clean off! The products aren't safe if they're exploding. Someone could have been hurt, and if they had, I never would have forgiven myself.
I've got to close. It's the only answer.

Cassie: Do that and you put a lot of people out of work, Van. You don't want to rush into a decision like that, especially when there's a chance the products weren't to blame.

Savannah: What do you mean?

Cassie: Like I said, the investigation is still ongoing but… The specialist they called in said it could be arson.

Savannah: What?!

Cassie: It's not a given, but it looks like the chemicals might have been tampered with. We should know more when they get results back from their lab in a few days.

Savannah: Who on earth would do such a thing? Put people in danger like that? I mean, I know some folks think it's scandalous to have a sex toy company at the edge of town, but…

Cassie: It's in the middle of town. Right by the post office.

Savannah: Well, yes, but the sign is very tasteful.

Cassie: The sign is a sun having an orgasm.

Savannah: She is not. She's just happy!

Cassie: Too happy.

Savannah: That's like saying babies are too cute or ice cream is too delicious or water slides are too much fun.

Cassie: I'm just playing devil's advocate here. And looking at it from the perspective of an older person who grew up in a less free-and-easy time… I can understand why they're freaked out. But that's no excuse for putting lives in danger. So if this is a case of sabotage, I'll hire security and make sure the factory is so closely guarded nothing like this will ever happen again.
In the meantime, we're back to business as usual tomorrow. We've moved product development to another space while we clean up the old lab and Ruthie May is going to bring in a box of Maud's famous Sunshine-inspired cookies from Dough on the Square to get everyone excited about a fresh start Tuesday morning.

Savannah: The vagina cookies or the penis ones?

Cassie: I…don't know. I didn't realize they were those kind of cookies.

Savannah: Oh, yeah, Maud is a big Sunshine fan, even if her husband is a stick in the mud who hates fun. She makes the most adorable sexy sugar cookies. The vagina ones have a little sugar pearl clitoris on them and everything!

Cassie: Oh God.

Savannah: What?

Cassie: Nothing. That's just kind of gross, isn't it?

Savannah: You ate penis lollipops at my bachelorette party without a problem. Don't you believe in equal representation of genitalia in baking and candy-making?

Cassie: What I believe is that you were meant to run this company and I can't wait for you to come home, rested and rejuvenated and ready to lead Sunshine Toys into a bright and shiny new future.

Savannah: Oh, sweet Cass. I love you, but this isn't like all the other times I've said I was running away from home. I have actually run away—I'm out of the country and loose in a foreign land—and I don't think I'm coming back anytime soon.
I'm so sorry to disappoint you. And my beautiful employees.
Maybe I should just give the company to Ruthie May and call it a day?

Cassie: No! Not Ruthie May. She would go mad given that much power. And drive the rest of Happy Cat crazy along with her. Plus, she keeps talking about retiring.

Savannah: Olivia?

Cassie: Eh…

Savannah: I know. She's a disaster, but I love her. She's been my bestie since we were eight years old. I couldn't *not* give her a job after her mom died.

Cassie: You've got a big heart. And that's why Steve's betrayal is tearing you apart right now. But big hearts don't just hurt big. They also heal big. Even bigger and better than they were before.

Savannah: How did you get so wise?

Cassie: I read a lot of books. And I've learned a lot from watching my kick-ass little sister. You've weathered break-ups and heartbreak before. You can do this. There's no doubt in my mind. I'll check in with you soon, okay? In the meantime try to have fun and see a few sights aside from the interior of every bakery in London.

Savannah: I'll try. Thank you for babysitting my life. Everything A-okay at the house, at least? You're comfortable and have everything you need?

Cassie: The house is great. I love being so close to the lake and the woods. I go hiking every morning before riding my sister's obnoxious dildo-handled bicycle to work.

Savannah: Lol. I would pay money to see you on my bike, my shy little squirrel.

Cassie: When you come home I'll ride it around the block for you. You can film it for posterity.

Savannah: If I come home.

Cassie: When.

Savannah: We'll see. Oh, and remember Tuesday is trash day so be sure to put the bins and the recycling out at the end of the drive. With the lids on tight and the rocks beside the mailbox on top.

Cassie: Already done. I told you, I've got this, lady. Don't worry about me. Everything is under control.

THREE

Cassie Sunderwell
(aka an overworked computer gamer geek who needs a vacation from her vacation)

EVERYTHING IS *NOT* UNDER CONTROL.

Everything is chaos and insanity and explosions and fires and intimidating sex toys—half of which I would have no idea how to use, even if I were of the mind to do that "product research" Savannah's been encouraging since she started making fake penises for a living—and now...him.

Him. Ryan O'Dell, Mr. Popular, star of the wrestling team, and voted Most Likely to Stay Hot For Eternity every year of high school.

Mr. Used-to-haunt-my-dreams.

Mr. And-he-did-again-last-night.

Not only has he *not* moved out of town, the way I'd naively assumed after not seeing him around Happy Cat my first week on the job as Savannah's temporary replacement, he's become a big, bossy firefighter with broad shoulders and a chiseled jaw and piercing blue eyes that have somehow gotten even bluer and more knee-weakeningly intense in the nine years since he broke my stupid teenage heart.

And the most pathetic part is that he clearly had no idea who I was…at least at first.

I'm as invisible to him as I was in high school. But at least now I know better than to think it means something when he looks at me *that* way, like he'd enjoy ripping my tee shirt off with his obnoxiously shiny and perfectly shaped white teeth.

Even if I have been accidentally thinking about him every minute since he showed up at Sunshine Toys yesterday…

Ryan's sex-eyes and the dreamy way he used to say my name—like he was Mozart and my name was his most triumphant creation—are nothing but his default attract mode. Like a video game screen saver set to play a tempting part of the game, designed to lure people in to spend their hard-earned money, Ryan is always on. He's a gorgeous man who enjoys attention and has adapted his code to draw in as much of it as possible.

If only I'd realized that sooner. But at sixteen I was so ridiculously innocent.

Compared to the sophisticated, experienced, sex-kitten-about-town you are now, the inner voice offers snidely as I gather this morning's empty cornflakes box and the toilet paper tube to take outside to add to the recycling bins.

"Shut up, inner voice," I mutter.

You wouldn't be so cranky if you'd gotten laid, it answers. *Like…ever.*

I grimace in response. Maybe I would've finally lost

this pesky V-card—seriously, it's a minus five charisma penalty—if I'd gone to SuperHero*Con like I was supposed to last week. I had my Captainess America costume all ready, and I'd been chatting in an online gamer group with *Flash185*, a fellow coder from Detroit with a quirky sense of humor and a decently cute profile pic, about having butter beer at the hotel bar one night. I *know* that could've gone somewhere between the sheets.

Maybe it would've been awkward and mortifying and I probably would have laughed at inappropriate times, but at least I would've finally entered the adulting levels of life.

And then maybe I wouldn't be having wild dreams starring Ryan O'Dell, dildos, and flaming sheets.

I step out the front door of Savannah's cottage, ducking under the massive *Steve The Cheater Doesn't Live Here Anymore* banner that she hung from the edge of the porch roof. After a week, it's started to blend in with the old live oaks and magnolias up and down the street, getting droopy and relaxed in the early June heat.

I should probably take it down. Fresh starts are important, and coming home to a sign bashing her ex won't help Savannah maintain the Zen she's finding in Europe.

My boots squish against the damp stone walk leading to the trash cans at the curb. This is the first time in two years that I've been back to Happy Cat, and I can't say I've missed the humid summers. I'll take San Francisco weather any day.

But San Francisco doesn't have hot firefighters, that inner voice pipes up.

"Pretty sure it does," I mutter back.

None that you've come close enough to sniff though.

And now I'm thinking about Ryan smelling like soap

and lemon and fire hose—yes, fire hose has a smell, and it's oddly sexy—and I'm silently persuading myself that there will be no more reasons for him to come to Sunshine Toys. I'll go to work and come straight home and our paths need never cross again. I therefore won't have to worry about how good he smells or how fine he looks or the way my heart makes like a fainting goat every time he shoots one of his signature sex-eye stares my way.

I reach the recycling bin, and the trash can next to it chirps at me.

I blink at the brown canister on wheels.

The lid thumps, and I shriek and jump back. The lid thumps again, and this time, two glittering black eyes peer out.

"*Aaaagh!*" I stumble backward, trip on the curb, and land on my ass as two furry paws appear. I crab-walk back toward the house, except—thanks to my job involving sitting on my ass twelve hours a day—I can't tie my shoes without getting winded. So basically there's a snail beating me, and that twinge of carpal tunnel in my right wrist is protesting being asked to bear the weight of my torso.

As I scuttle sluggishly away, a raccoon pulls himself from the trash bin, wearing Savannah's broken string of Christmas lights and dragging a bag of leftover penis lollipops from her bachelorette party that I was helpfully trying to dispose of.

"Drop it," I hiss, slipping in the slick grass as I try to get back on my feet.

Can raccoons have rabies? And if so, is this one looking rabid? Or is that gleam in his eyes normal for a masked bandit?

He eyes my boots. I glance down, and the sparkly

Thor hammer I tied to my laces for inspiration glitters up at me.

"Back," I say as sternly as I can, because there's no way I'm beating a raccoon in a foot race unless he trips on that string of Christmas lights.

He leaps to the ground and takes three steps toward me. I crab-walk two steps back. His beady eyes are trained on my shoes, and since I only play a superhero online or at gaming conventions, this isn't looking good.

Maybe if I pry my boot off, I can fling it at him and make a dash for the door?

I reach for my laces and, swear on my PlayStation 4, he smirks and rubs his palms together like a super villain. As if he's looking forward to adding my Skecher to his armful of spoils as soon as I toss it over.

This is what I get for drinking decaf. It's like diet coffee, and who wants to sacrifice the best part of coffee? I need my caffeine.

And more exercise.

And for this raccoon to act like I'm a scary human and run away.

He tosses the penis lollipops like they're last year's hard drives and he has his eye on this year's double-core processors.

"No, you want the lollipops," I tell him. "They taste so much better than Thor's hammer, I promise."

He skitters closer.

I shriek and kick at him. He pauses, but only for a beat before he picks up the pace. Because, dummy me, my flailing is just making the sparkly thing on my boot flash more.

The only other weapons at hand are some pocket lint and damp grass clippings, and I somehow doubt hurling either of those will slow him down. Even if I had a rock or a garden gnome on hand, it wouldn't make much of a difference. Back in high school, I could fire a softball from third base at sixty-four miles per hour, but I'm so out of practice I almost strained my shoulder tossing a wad of paper into the recycling bin last week.

Which means I have exactly one option left.

"Help!" I yell. "*Help! Rabid raccoon!*"

The raccoon chitters back accusingly.

"*I* didn't do anything wrong," I protest. "*You're* the one stealing my garbage and getting aggressive about it."

I swear the little monster rolls his eyes before hunching down in prelude to a pounce. I'm bracing myself to have my eyes clawed out when a calm voice behind me says, "George, back off."

A calm, masculine, I dreamt-about-that-sexy-rumble-all-night voice…

The raccoon pauses.

My heart doesn't. It slams against my ribs while I tell myself that's not Ryan behind me. It's his voice twin. Someone who sounds exactly like him. And who smells like soap and lemon and fire hose and can control raccoons with his varmint-whispering skills.

"Put the anal beads back and stay out of Savannah's trash," he continues.

I gape at the Christmas lights draped around the raccoon's body.

No wonder I couldn't find the outlet plug.

The raccoon—George, apparently—shuffles back around to the other side of the trash can and reclaims the penis lollipops, but makes no move to put the *anal beads* draped over his shoulders back in the trash.

I turn slowly, first noting that there's a black truck parked in the driveway next door that I haven't seen before.

And now there's a big, broad, sleepy-eyed Ryan O'Dell bending over me. "You okay? George is mostly harmless. Likes shiny things, though."

He offers a hand, and I eyeball his long, blunt fingers.

"You know the raccoon," I say, easing out of my crab-crawl position. My back twinges sharply, and I wonder if I should add yoga or something to my daily hikes around the lake while I'm here on vacation.

"George Cooney? We go way back. He adopted me when he was just a kit." We both look back at the raccoon, who grins as he waddles around to Ryan's side. "Did Savannah mention the rocks on the cans? That helps keep him out of the trash."

"Oh. The *big* rocks."

"Yeah. The *big* rocks. We learned that the hard way after she tossed out a bunch of half-melted dildos last year. George planted them in our vegetable garden. Was real torn up when they didn't grow."

"Did you remember to fertilize them regularly?"

He laughs, that easy rumble of his that always made me feel ten times funnier than I am.

But I'm *not* funny. Ryan just likes to laugh. He has the easy-going charm thing down pat, which was part of the reason I didn't recognize his voice right away yesterday. The Tough Firefighter tone coming from him was a surprise.

A sexy surprise, that I do my best *not* to think about as Ryan says, "No, we didn't. That must have been where we went wrong. But we ended up with a bumper crop of cucumbers. Hoping for the same this year. You're welcome to grab a few once they get ripe." He hooks a thumb at the cottage next door with a wink that turns my panties inside out. "Now, come on, let me help you up."

He holds his hand out again, fingers spread wide to

reveal white scar tissue between his right thumb and forefinger. It's something new, like that faint white line on his cheek, and it sends a jolt of worry through my chest. Fighting fires is a dangerous job and no matter how deeply this man mortified me when we were kids, I don't like the idea of him being in danger.

I don't like it one little bit.

"You okay?" he asks.

"Fine. I'm fine." I scramble to my feet on my own, feeling like a fool.

Clearly, Ryan O'Dell still gets under my skin.

And Savannah should've warned me about her neighbor.

"Cool. Large rocks. Cucumbers. Got it." I dust my butt as his gaze dips down to my chest, and I realize I'm wearing my *Space Vikings Invade Butte* game launch party tee.

The one the printer screwed up that reads *Space Vikings Invade Butt* instead.

I clamp my arms over my chest, trying desperately to cover the worst of it without being too obvious. I love a goofy tee as much as the next girl, but not in front of this man, who already thinks I'm the saddest nerd ever to crawl out from under an old Atari. "I'm sure Savannah will be back soon. I won't have the chance to mess up the trash much longer."

"You think she's coming home that fast?"

No. "Of course. She's having a fabulous time abroad, but she misses Happy Cat and the office."

Even the raccoon gives me the *yeah, right, crazy lady* eyeball while it rubs against Ryan's leg like a cat.

He grunts. "Interesting. She mentioned selling it before she left."

Dammit. I hate hearing that—more evidence that

Savannah might be serious about giving up on Sunshine Toys.

But she was born to run this company. Some people think she peaked professionally before *Savannah Sunshine* went off the air—Van played a child sleuth in the hit series for eight years, and yes, there are pitfalls to being the sister of a Hollywood starlet—but there's more in her big heart and amazing brain than acting talent. She's truly passionate about helping women lead sex- and pleasure-positive lives. She was outraged when she learned that eleven percent of women in the U.S. have *never* had an orgasm and vowed to right that heinous wrong or die trying.

Van's the Joan of Arc of sex toys. It's a calling for her, one she's going to come back to—I hope.

"She also mentioned taking out billboards from Atlanta to Orlando with pictures of Steve below the headline *Cheating Bastard*," I point out to Ryan. "But she didn't. She's coming back, and everything will be fine."

"Uh-huh." He nods carefully. "Well, if it's not, let me know if I can help out in any way. Savannah's a good neighbor and friend. I hate that things ended so badly for her and Steve."

I snort. "I'm not. I got bad vibes from that man the moment I met him. I thought I had to be wrong, because she was so happy, but apparently not. I'm glad he's out of her life for good."

Ryan's shoulders slump in what looks like relief. "Right? Me too. He makes my skin crawl."

I nod with unconcealed enthusiasm, too thrilled to meet someone else who wasn't blindsided by Steve's misbehavior to play it cool. "Yes! Right off my body. It's something in his eyes or his sneaky little mouth or—" I break off with a shudder. "I don't know, but it's wrong. It's all wrong."

"Preaching to the choir, Sunderwell." Ryan lifts a palm in the air in a silent amen. "But people around here think he hung the moon for keeping the biggest bank in town from closing a few years ago so I figured my gut was wrong."

I shake my head. "Nope. Your gut was dead on."

"Your gut and my gut," he says, lips curving on one side. "Sound like they've got more in common than a person might think."

"Yeah, well," I laugh, suddenly acutely uncomfortable. "Every microbiome is its own unique universe, so probably not, but…"

He frowns. " A micro what?"

"Biome. It's the, um…combined genetic material of the microbes living in our gut that aid in digestion and other metabolic activity. They're a counterpart to our genetic material, but actually outnumber the genes in our own genome by about a hundred to one, so…"

Ryan's lips turn down as he nods. "Wow."

He sounds as unimpressed by my nerd vomit as his raccoon, who has flopped onto his back and is tugging at the hem of Ryan's jeans as if to say, "Please can we ditch the geek, and go home and feast upon peen lollies together in manly silence?"

Ugh!

What am I even doing standing here talking to Ryan O'Dell? Who cares if we happen to see eye-to-eye on one stupid thing? Ryan and I have about as much in common as Space Vikings and vegan buffalo chicken wings, and I have a new exercise routine to keep up with. Every second spent chit-chatting with him is a second I'm not walking around the lake getting fit.

"So, anyway, have fun with your raccoon. And Van's trash." I stand up straighter. "I should get going."

He's still watching me with that intense gaze that keeps dropping to my shirt.

Or my lips?

I probably have a milk mustache or something. That's my life since I came back to my hometown, one embarrassing interlude after another, interspersed with occasional explosions.

I turn to make my escape into the woods, where no one will care what I'm wearing or how sloppily I ate my cornflakes, when Ryan speaks again.

"Good to see you again, Cassie."

Damn it. I might not be teenage Cassie anymore, and he's *definitely* not teenage Ryan, but the way my body reacts to my name on his lips is exactly the same. He still has the power to make me melt on command.

Another reason to get out of here. Now.

I can't let myself take a single step down the road to Crushville with this man. I refuse to set myself up for a refresher course in heartbreak.

So I just nod at him before I tromp back to the trailhead with my head held high.

"Being hot as a fire truck doesn't make him worth wasting one second of your time," I whisper to myself. "You've got better things to do than mess with Ryan O'Dell."

Liar, my inner voice replies.

I need a new inner voice.

FOUR

Ryan

THE WILD HOG is as exciting as it ever is on a Tuesday night. Some rednecks with more beer in their bellies than sense are fighting in the corner over who cheated at pool. Emma June, Ruthie May's granddaughter, and her on-again-off-again boyfriend, Tucker, are apparently on tonight, making out in their usual booth by the bathrooms. And Ruthie May is holding court with the Happy Cat Gossip Queens at two tables pushed together in the center of the room.

Meanwhile my little brother—the oldest of my three younger brothers—is behind the bar, scowling while he yanks the taps and tops off Coke glasses. Jace glances my way, adds a *don't start, jackass* sneer to his bad attitude, and disappears into the kitchen.

I make my way through the bar, answering questions about yesterday's lube fire, which will be a hot topic in

Happy Cat until something more exciting happens. Like Sunshine Toys releasing their holiday line-up or a new petition to kick the company out of town starts circulating. We used to fight about installing windmills by the highway or who cooks the best catfish, but lately, it's been all Sunshine drama all the time.

And, as usual, the town's split on whether the fire was karmic retribution for the shamelessly perverted or simply an unfortunate accident.

I claim a stool far away from Olivia, who's at the other end of the bar entertaining three-quarters of the single men in town between the ages of twenty and fifty. Probably reading their chakras or adjusting their auras or something.

More power to her.

Them, too. I don't always understand her and her new-age mumbo jumbo, but I've never known Olivia to say a bad word about anybody, or even bless anybody's heart. Not in the backward insult kind of way, anyway. What she lacks in Southern education she makes up for in sheer enthusiasm, and there are worse ways to while away an evening than with a friendly woman who likes to smile a lot, even if she may have been short-changed in the common sense department. At least she has good intentions, which is more than I can say for some of the other people in this town.

She waves.

I wave back.

And Jace slaps a bottle of Blue Moon on the bar in front of me with more force than absolutely necessary.

I arch a brow. "That aromatherapy spritzer Olivia worked up for your temper seems to be working."

"It was for my heart chakra, jackass," he says with attitude that's over the top, even for Jace.

I lean in, adding in a softer voice, "Whoa, hey. Something happen today?"

"Nothing I want your opinion on." Jace heads back down the bar to grab an empty burger basket without further comment, and I stifle a sigh.

Jace has been stuck in the same pattern with the same woman since high school, and about every four months, like clockwork, it gives me a nasty case of heartburn. All I've ever wanted is to see all three of my brothers happy. It eats at me that I can't fix Jace's bad habit. And hooking up again and again with a woman whose favorite form of entertainment is seeing how close she can get to cheating on him before he explodes is a bad habit, not love, no matter what anyone else has to say about it.

The fact that Ginger is a kindergarten teacher doesn't automatically mean she's sweet, innocent, or "too good" for my rough-around-the-edges brother. She's trouble, the sneaky kind that slips under most people's radar and makes her all the more dangerous because of it.

Why am I the only person in town who sees this shit clearly?

Even Jessie, my chief and a woman whose judgment I admire in most areas, seems taken in by Ginger's game.

It's like with Steve, Savannah's ex. Just because he's a good-looking high school football star turned banker prodigy, people think he's the catch of the fucking town.

Or they did until he got caught balls deep in a sheep. But even now it's clear some people think there must have been some kind of mistake. I've heard a few people say that Savannah wasn't seeing things clearly. Or that she was making the whole thing up. Or maybe the sheep was asking for it, walking around, all freshly shorn and showing off its hindquarters in that field after dark.

No wonder she left town.

Cassie is the first person I've met who pegged Steve as fast as I did.

It makes me curious what she would say about Ginger. I'd ask her, but given her cool dismissal this morning, I'm guessing she's not interested in more than a civil neighborly relationship. Plus, Jace would be pissed. He already knows how I feel about Ginger, and asking an outsider's opinion won't help my case.

The door opens, and the savvy brunette herself breezes into the bar.

Cassie's bouncy brown pigtails are ridiculously cute, and a wayward part of me is instantly dying to know how they'd feel wrapped around my hands. Knowing my luck she's probably wearing one of those sexy-as-hell tee shirts of hers, and I'll be fighting to keep my gaze above her neck for the rest of the night.

I cast a subtle glance south of her pretty smile as she waves at Ruthie May, and sure enough—this time she's wearing a vintage Ms. Pac-Man tee, the character posed seductively on top of chunky letters. And though I've never found a yellow ball wearing lipstick sexy in the slightest, I can't stop staring.

But of course it isn't Ms. Pacman that gets to me. Or the shirt. It's the woman in the shirt, the curvy, sweet-smelling, adorably serious woman who has been running through my mind pretty much constantly since I made an idiot of myself this morning trying—and failing—to offer intelligent commentary on her scientific thoughts about the microbial life in the human gut.

I'm no dummy, but I was a welder before I joined the department. I've never darkened a hall of higher learning. I was too busy busting my ass to help my parents put food on the table right out of high school to have the time, or the money, to go to college.

Most days, that doesn't bother me much. I love being a firefighter and I'm proud of the sacrifices I made so that my younger brothers could have choices I didn't have. But sometimes, I wish I'd had more opportunity to stretch my brain and people to talk to who know more about the world outside of Happy Cat.

"I assume you want the chicken sandwich," Jace says from behind me. He's dialed down the bitter, but his voice still makes me flinch as I shift my attention his way. "And a side of fries, as usual," he continues.

I frown. "Am I that predictable?"

Jace sighs through his nose in response, making me frown harder.

"No, thank you," I say, rolling my shoulders back. Here I am wishing for something more, but sticking to old patterns and habits too. "I'll have the buffalo wing salad with ranch instead of blue cheese dressing and an order of fried okra on the side."

"The okra's not in yet," Jace says flatly. "But I've got fried squash blossoms. They're good."

"I'll take those. And cobbler for dessert, whatever's freshest." I point a finger his way as inspiration strikes. "Two orders, please. Send the first order over now. To the brunette at table three."

Brows shooting up, Jace glances over my shoulder. "Ruthie May?"

I frown. "No. The other brunette. The cute one who's not old enough to be my mother."

His brows creep even higher, and the prickly-ass attitude disappears completely. "Cassie Sunderwell?" Jace whistles low, shifting his attention back to me. "Trying to mend fences?"

"What? Why? You mean because of the fire? There

wasn't any water damage. And even if there had been, that's hardly my fault."

"No, I don't mean the fire," Jace says in a tone that implies I must have already had a few too many. "I mean she hates you. Or she hated you in high school, anyway."

My frown becomes a full-fledged scowl. "What? No, she didn't. Cassie and I were friends."

Jace snorts.

"We were," I insist. "We had English together."

Our English project was the highlight of the last semester of my senior year. I looked forward to the afternoons we spent rehearsing our scene from *Romeo and Juliet* every day, a bright spot in my busy studying, working, keeping-a-younger-sibling-from-killing-himself-until-my-parents-got-home life.

Until we were cast opposite each other, I'd assumed Cassie was shy—she didn't speak up much in class—but that wasn't the case at all. She was smart and confident and, once she opened up a little, really funny.

God, she made me laugh. And kissing her was weirdly nice too, even though it was just pretend for the play and she seemed so young back then it was hard to believe she was actually sixteen. With her hair always in a ponytail, big glasses, and oversized clothing, she looked about twelve.

At eighteen, that'd made me a little uncomfortable about our mini make-out scene, but still…there was something there. Something that made me sad when the scene was over, even though we got an A.

"You might've had English together, but you didn't have anything else together," my brother tells me.

He's not making any sense. "We got close," I insist quietly. "We did a project together my senior year. She was so smart they put her in senior English when she was only a sophomore, remember?"

My brother rolls his eyes. "Yes, I remember. I was a sophomore then too, dude. My friends knew her friends and I was there at the softball end-of-season keg party when she got drunk and told everyone who would listen that she hated Ryan O'Dell like festering wart-boils."

I wince. "Festering wart-boils?"

"No one likes festering wart-boils."

"Clearly." My shoulders slump. "Shit."

"Yeah," Jace says, his expression softening. "But whatever. Who cares? Everyone knows the Sunderwell girls are a little out there."

"Do they?" I ask, my jaw going tight. "Don't you ever get tired of what 'everyone in this town' knows? Don't you ever just want to jump out of the damned Happy Cat mentality and think for yourself?"

Jace's gaze darkens again, but he doesn't respond right away. His focus slides to the table behind me, lingering for a long moment, before coming back to rest on my face. "I'll get the cobbler, but you take it over to her yourself. Look into her eyes while you do it and be honest with yourself about what you see. That's part of the trouble with this town too, you know."

"What's that?" I ask, shocked to get this many words in a row out of Jace, especially when he's in a foul mood.

"What 'everyone knows.'" His lips twist in a smirk. "The person in the mirror is part of that too, isn't it? People in this town like to tell you who you are. Makes thinking for yourself harder than it sounds."

I nod slowly, impressed. And hopeful. Maybe my little brother isn't going to stay chained to a woman who treats him like shit for the rest of his life. Maybe he's going to break out of the mold this town poured him into the day he got arrested for racing dirt bikes through the golf course freshman year and forge a new path for himself.

Reaching out, I clap a hand on his shoulder. "I'm proud of you."

Jace rolls his eyes. "You want the cobbler or not?"

I glance over my shoulder to see Cassie laughing with her co-workers, her eyes dancing in a free, easy way they didn't when we were alone together this morning, and my chest tightens.

I turn back to Jace. "No cobbler."

"She might like cobbler." He shrugs. "Only one way to find out."

I push my beer back across the bar toward him and slide off my stool. "Nah, not tonight, little brother. See you later."

"No dinner? I can get it wrapped to go."

I shake my head as I head toward the rear exit, down the hall by the supply closet, determined not to attract Cassie's attention while she's enjoying herself. I want to know what I did wrong so I can make it right, but I'm not going to put her on the spot in public.

I am, however, going to prove to her that I'm not a bad guy and that we should be friends again. We're neighbors, after all. For now.

With one last glance at her table, and that smile that makes me want to know Cassie again more than I want sleep after a double shift, I head for home.

There, I find George chasing a vibrator—turned on, no pun intended—around my screened-in porch. After making sure he's not going to accidentally electrocute himself if he bites through the outer case, I make a batch of vegetable quesadillas and contemplate the mysteries of the universe with a cold beer and a copy of my high school yearbook spread open on the kitchen table. But staring at Cassie's sixteen-year-old face doesn't offer any answers. Not to why she apparently hated me then, or to why it matters so much that I get to know her again now.

Whatever I did, I want to clear the air. I want to fix it.

But I can't fix it if she won't talk to me.

I point my last quesadilla triangle at George, who's lounging on the couch in the other room, petulantly eating grapes because I refused to make him popcorn. "I need a plan, George. What I really need is a plan."

FIVE

Cassie

BECAUSE OF SAVANNAH'S schedule filming *Savannah Sunshine* when we were kids, we usually spent five months a year in California before coming home for most of the school year. Life in Happy Cat was our parents' way of inserting as much normalcy into our lives as possible. We had tutors to keep us on track while Savannah was on set, of course, but most of her work was done between May and September.

I didn't do Georgia summers until high school, after her show ended its run.

Wednesday is one more reminder why I choose not to do Georgia summers now. I'm wilting like a plump sunflower and stealing ice chips from Sunshine Toys' sno-cone stand at the farmers' market in Sunshine Square to keep from passing out in the heat.

The square was named for Savannah's TV show. Not

her sex toy factory. And that should really be the full name of the square, because it's how all the locals refer to it now. *Sunshine Square, named for the Savannah Sunshine TV show, not for…you know.*

Even Ruthie May makes the distinction, and she's the proudest local employee Savannah has. She's explaining it to an out-of-towner who came by for the weekly market right now, as a matter of fact.

"Oh, yes. Savannah Sunshine is a local. She's done so much good for our community, and we're so proud of *everything* she's accomplished. Sno-cone? Savannah insists we hand them out for free. It's just common decency in this dadgum heat."

"We have mango-lime, strawberry surprise, and cherry," Olivia adds. She's positively glowing in the late afternoon humidity. I don't know if it's her aura cleansing ritual or what, but if it weren't for that paper fan she's waving on her face, I wouldn't believe she's even noticed the heat. She's fresh as the morning dew in her adorable short jean shorts, bangles on both wrists, big sunglasses that hide half her face, and a sun hat over her blond braids.

She looks like a Southern belle the way she's working that fan, and it *does* have the Sunshine Toys logo on it, so she might actually be a marketing genius in disguise.

Our customers all pick the strawberry surprise, and we load them up with sno-cones before sending them down to check out the fresh corn on the cob a few booths over.

"Really smart to theme the sno-cone flavors to match the summer lube flavors," I tell Olivia.

I'm working on not blushing when I say *lube*. The fact that my face is already emulating a sweating cherry in the heat is definitely working to my advantage at winning this battle. High-five to me. I pop another ice chunk in my mouth.

"Oh, we didn't just theme them," Olivia says brightly. "We're flavoring the sno-cones with the actual lube."

The ice gets caught in my throat, and Ruthie May smacks me on the back until it goes flying over our table and lands on a local farmer's back. I wince, but the man in the overalls doesn't seem to notice the ice already melting into his clothes, so I don't bother to apologize.

I have bigger problems than assault with a chunk of sno-cone.

"What? We can't use—" I rasp before another coughing fit hits me.

"But we use all natural ingredients," Olivia explains while I try to get rid of the itch clawing at my throat. "Completely edible."

"I thought the coconut oil would solidify on the ice, but Neil tweaked the formula so it's working perfectly," Ruthie May adds. "Going down real smooth."

"*Stop*," I gasp between coughs. If any of the town prudes hear that we're spreading Satan's sex juice all over innocent children's sno-cones, we'll get investigated by the health department. I'll have to tell Savannah about it, and she will *absolutely* sell the company.

I have to do something. Stat!

I'm bent double, hacking out my tonsils while I rack my brain, when a raccoon on a leash stops in front of our table.

The hairs on the top of my head prickle just like the hairs on my nape stood up at the Wild Hog last night when I was failing miserably at *not* being oh-so-aware of Ryan sitting at the bar, looking delicious in faded jeans and a tight blue tee shirt the same pristine mountain lake shade as his eyes.

I blame Ruthie May for that too.

She kept whispering that he was looking at me until he left.

"You okay, Cassie?" Ryan asks.

"Oh my gosh, Ryan, thank the goddess you're here," Olivia says while I try not to cough-spit on Ryan's shoes. Or his raccoon. "I think she needs the Heimlich."

Metal clinks, and an open stainless-steel water bottle appears under my nose. Two more points to Ryan for being environmentally friendly. "Here," he says, "take a drink. George doesn't mind sharing."

I'm too grateful for the water to get mad that he's offering me his raccoon's water. I gulp the cool liquid, spilling some down my favorite *Firefly* tee shirt.

"Thank you," I say when I'm finally able to talk without hacking up a lung.

And that's when I make the fatal mistake.

I look him straight in the eye, and the raw concern in the furrow of his brows melts into one of those friendly smiles that flips my belly inside out and renders me incapable of using my tongue for speech. Though I'm pretty sure I could work up the lingual fortitude to lick several parts of him — repeatedly.

Why does he have this effect on me? Even after being responsible for the most mortifying moment of my entire life, he still makes me swoon like I did that time Wil Wheaton told me he liked my Supergirl costume at Comic-Con.

In California, I learned to expect that people might not be what they pretend to be on the surface. Yes, I was young, but my parents were like hawks on set, and they made sure Savannah and I knew not to trust the boys — or sometimes men — who hinted at wanting to spend time alone with us.

But I thought Ryan, at least, was one of the good guys, and that I wouldn't find Hollywood-level deception in Happy Cat.

He proved me wrong.

He proved me *so* wrong.

And if the Ryan O'Dells of the world are secretly backstabbing creeps, then what hope is there for any other man?

"Better?" he asks.

I want to believe that honest, friendly concern is real, but I have trust issues.

And they're his fault.

"Yes." My voice is all kinds of raspy and unattractive, but it doesn't matter, because I refuse to care if I'm attractive to Ryan. "Thank you."

I hand him back his bottle and wipe my sweaty palms on my shorts.

He scans me up and down, but I remind myself it's professional firefighter Ryan making sure I'm okay, and that the fact that my skin tingles under my clothes everywhere he looks would mean nothing to him. This attraction is not a reciprocal problem.

"That's so sweet of you to take care of Cassie," Olivia says. "You two are just adorable, and not just because you have complimentary auras. Which reminds me, Cassie, I need to do your birth chart this week." She sighs dreamily. "Aren't they adorable, Ruthie May?"

Ruthie May perks up like a shark that's smelled blood in the water. "Well, I reckon they are." She shoots a look between Ryan and me, and I can already see heads twisting. The entire town can sense when Ruthie May gets her teeth sunk into a new story. She lets off gossip pheromones.

"George is the adorable one," I say, because the

raccoon is kinda cute. When he's not wearing anal beads and lifting penis pops out of Savannah's trash can. "How are we doing on ice? Do we need more? I can go pick up more if we're running short."

"We have plenty," Ruthie May says without looking, so I lean over and look in the cooler.

"Oh, we do, don't we?"

"And we have plenty of lu—"

"FLAVORING!" I yell over Olivia. "We should get grape flavoring too. I love grape."

"But we don't have any—"

"Exactly. Grape flavored flavoring is important."

Ryan's smiling at all of us like we're highly amusing, albeit a little crazy. "I like lemonade on my cone," he says.

"*Ooooh,*" Ruthie May and Olivia say together.

"I'll text Savannah," Olivia adds.

"Psh," Ruthie May replies. "Don't bother her. We can handle this on our own. Cassie, we need you to approve lemonade-flavored lube."

"Approved," I say, desperate to change the subject before my already flaming cheeks ignite with embarrassment. "Can we—"

"Help! *HELP!*" a terrified young voice shrieks from the other side of the market.

I turn to see the two teen girls who just snagged sno-cones from our booth dropping to their knees on the ground beside the glass blowing booth. Ryan takes off at a run, leaving George Cooney's leash in Olivia's mostly-capable hands. After a beat of hesitation, I race after him, in a huffing-and-puffing, can't-keep-up-with-fit-people kind of way.

I don't know exactly why I'm running, except I have this awful feeling that I need to go. I need to see what's happened. I need to make sure everyone is okay. Maybe it's paranoia, but between the fire at the factory and the fear that someone will find out we're serving lubed-up sno-cones, my control issues are revved up in a major way.

One of the teenagers—the brunette with the curly ponytail—is pawing through her mother's purse. Her younger sister is crying. Their mother is on the ground, clutching at her throat while her cheeks turn red. She fights to pull in a breath while her eyes stream tears and a crowd gathers.

By the time I reach the scene, Ryan's already at the mother's side, talking calmly to one of the girls. "Coconut," Curly Ponytail says. "She's allergic to coconut."

My lungs freeze, and a slow panic builds in my chest.

Coconut. Coconut oil is the base ingredient in all of Savannah's lube.

And it was all over the sno-cones. I quickly scan the area, spotting three half-empty sno-cone sleeves in the grass not two feet away.

Ryan grabs the mom's purse and dumps it out beside the suffering woman. It only takes him a minute to find what he's looking for—an Epi-Pen.

Before I can look away, Ryan rips off the top of the needle and jabs it firmly into the woman's thigh, hard enough for it to punch through her jeans into her skin, all while murmuring to her in a comforting way completely at odds with his assertive jabbing.

Swallowing hard, I press a fist to my chest and ignore the woozy spinning of my head, willing myself not to pass out as I remind myself that not all needles are evil. Some needles save lives, like this one.

Still, I'm grateful when Ryan glances over his shoulder, looking relieved to see me, and says, "Cassie, call 9-1-1."

I nod and hurry to do his bidding, so glad that he's here. He just saved this woman's life.

After my team and I put it in horrible danger.

Throat tight with regret, I tug my phone from my back pocket and place the emergency call.

SIX

Cassie

FOUR HOURS LATER, I'm staring at my phone in Savannah's serene living room, willing the device to tell me that I don't really have to fill Savannah in on what InstaChat has already dubbed the Sunshine Sno Lube Disaster.

Despite the spa-like atmosphere with the comfy loungers, soft lighting, lavender-vanilla diffusers, and mood music that pipes in every night from seven to midnight like magic—apparently Olivia gave the room a makeover as a divorce present—my blood pressure is around the same stage it was last month at work when our team discovered a bug in *Space Vikings Invade Butte* forty-eight hours before launch.

We fixed the game.

But I don't know if I can fix everything that's falling apart at Savannah's company.

It's not just the lube fire or the farmers' market disaster. Morale is low and shipments are behind schedule, and I don't know how to fix it. I'm not used to dealing with people or products. I'm a code squirrel who lurks in my cozy den until my portion of the project is complete before emerging to troubleshoot with the other squirrels. I spend maybe *ten* percent of my job interacting IRL and the rest chatting with my team via video call or, better yet, while we're killing zombies in some post-apocalyptic virtual city. I am completely out of my element in Savannah's closely connected, highly collaborative work environment.

I miss San Francisco.

I miss my condo and my game set-up in my spare bedroom, with the PS4 and the dual-core tower.

I miss going three hours without someone mentioning something to do with sex and reminding me I've never had any.

And I miss being able to text my sister without mentioning a lube incident or having to assure her that no one at her company has died. *Yet.*

I can't let everything fall apart while she's gone. Even if she's serious about selling, no one will want Sunshine if it has a string of misfortunes hanging around its neck.

Someone knocks on my door, and I cringe.

Please don't be the mayor. Or Gerald Hutchins. Or Olivia.

Bless her heart, Olivia tries, and I love her almost as much as I love Savannah, but I really don't want to know what's going on with my star chart. As far as I'm concerned it's pretty obvious I was born under a bad sign.

When I fling open the door, I'm ready to shout *No comment!* and slam it shut — Ruthie May texted that there were some paparazzi in Atlanta who occasionally come down to Happy Cat if something's going on with Savannah, since she's still a public figure—but the sight of Ryan throws me off my game.

I immediately glance down at his feet for the raccoon. The last time I saw George Cooney, he was sliding down Main Street on his fuzzy butt, assisted by mango-lime lube he'd liberated from a pump bottle during the near-death commotion with the allergic tourist.

But the trash panda troublemaker is nowhere to be found. "George Cooney hitting the sack early tonight?"

"George is off on a walkabout," he says. "But he'll be back, I'm not worried."

I lift my gaze back to Ryan's face, taking in the view on the way. The man looks ridiculously gorgeous in a soft gray tee shirt and faded black jeans. Damn… Biceps like his should be illegal. Or at least come with a warning—likely to induce unexpected drooling in women, gay men, and basically anyone with a pulse.

Ryan lifts a sweating mason jar of something that looks suspiciously like homemade lemonade. "Thought you could use a pick-me-up. You holding up okay? You went a little pale when needles entered the picture today."

He's watching me like he's not sure if I'm going to fall apart or tell him where he can stick his lemonade, and something about the uncertainty is a kick to the gut.

Neither of us are the same people we were in high school. And he can't hurt me again, because I'm leaving to go back to my normal life in San Francisco.

As soon as Savannah gets back.

Which will hopefully be before I run out of vacation time at work.

I give him a small smile. "I'm not the one who almost died, so I think I'm pretty okay."

"She wasn't going to die."

"Not on your watch?"

"No, not on my watch." He grins, oozing with self-confidence, making him about ten thousand watts hotter than he was two seconds ago.

I remind myself that he can't help that he was born with a smile that could ignite a thousand panties and a natural charm that makes him popular without even trying. But I *can* control how close I let him.

Though surely there's nothing wrong with accepting a friendly lemonade.

I mean, he brought it all the way over from his house to mine. And he's checking on me, when it's basically my fault that a woman went into anaphylactic shock at the farmers' market—not to mention what happened to his raccoon—so maybe we can be friends.

Because this is ridiculously sweet of him.

I open the door wider and accept the lemonade. "Thank you. Did you want to…" I gesture inside.

His smile broadens, and he steps past me into the house. "Sure. Thanks."

"I'm sorry about George running off," I say.

Ryan takes a seat on a lavender settee, legs spread wide, holding his own mason jar. "He really will be back," he assures me. "The leash is just for show when he follows me out of the neighborhood. Special town ordinance just for George."

I shouldn't be surprised, but my eyebrows still shoot up.

He laughs. "Been in San Francisco so long you forgot how things work around here?"

"Apparently." I sip the lemonade. The sweet, tangy liquid hits my tongue, and my eyes slide shut. "Oh, wow, this is delicious."

"Yeah?"

"Please tell me it's not iced lube."

He laughs. "Not unless my grandma was way ahead of her time. Old family recipe."

"Right. That makes way more sense." I take a big gulp, because *wow*, this really is the best lemonade I've had in years.

"Don't tell me they don't have lemonade in San Francisco."

"Not like this. But they have sourdough bread and Peet's Coffee on every corner, so I get by."

"You like it out there?" He's watching me with that friendly grin, his gaze occasionally dipping down to my breasts, and I glance down too, just to make sure I'm not dribbling anything.

I appear to be in the clear, but I refuse to read anything into his wandering gaze or the fact that he knows where I live. I'd think it was weirder if he didn't. Even I can tell you where ninety percent of my graduating class and all their siblings ended up after high school. It's a Happy Cat thing. We gossip.

"I do like it," I tell him. "There's a ton to do in the city, I'm an hour from wine country, and the weather's perfect all year round. At least for me. I love jackets and unpredictable fog."

He smiles, appearing amused and bemused at the same time. "That's all it takes to make you happy?"

Maybe it's the lip-loosening lemonade effect, or those blue eyes I've never fully been able to resist, but I find myself telling him more than my standard answer. "Well, no. I miss being close to family. But Mom and Dad retired to Florida last year, so it's just Savannah here, and I like the anonymity of the city. Between all the press when we were kids, and the gossip here, it's nice to be in a place where nobody cares who I am. My coworkers are awesome. We all get super spun up when we're in the early stages of putting a new game together, or when we're launching, or when we're battling the bugs in the trenches." I shrug. "I *fit* there. We can hit a comedy club or a gaming convention or a concert without driving an hour into Atlanta and battling for parking. The mass transit system is so much better. Not perfect, but…." I trail off, suddenly keenly aware that I've been word-vomiting all over him. "Sorry. I'm being boring, aren't I?"

He shakes his head with a wistful sigh. "Not at all. It sounds amazing. I wish I knew what that felt like. That kind of…freedom."

What? What was that in his tone? It couldn't be *jealousy*? No way. Surely not. I am a person who *experiences* that emotion, not one who inspires it in others. "Well, it has its downsides, too. Parking is the worst and if I have to watch one more naked dude cruising the Tenderloin on his bicycle, I'm going to take to wearing a blindfold full time."

Ryan grins. "Seriously? They ride their bikes naked?"

"They do," I confirm. "But most of them wear a helmet so at least one head is protected."

He laughs harder this time, letting out a rich, lovely rumble that makes me feel warm all over.

"San Francisco is one of a kind." I lift a shoulder and take another sip of the lemonade. "But it's awesome here, too."

He hums dubiously and I wince, because even I don't believe me.

"Give it a day." He winks, and tingles race across my skin in response. "Tomorrow Maud and Gerald will get into it over her sexy cookies or someone's goat will get loose in town hall and the farmers' market will be forgotten."

"Maybe. But I don't think Happy Cat will *ever* forget

that Savannah opened a sex toy factory here. I've only been home a week and a half, and I've already heard at least a hundred opinions about Sunshine Toys." My phone dings, I glance down, and then I lift it to show him. "See?"

It's a text from Gerald Hutchins informing me that if the mayor won't shut down Savannah's company, he's going to the health department, because it's in the best interest of the health of the youth of our community not to be subjected to sex on a daily basis.

Ryan rolls his eyes. "You know how much tax money the town gets from that factory? No one's going to shut her down."

I sigh, wishing I had ten percent of his faith that this was all going to blow over. "I admire her so much for putting the factory front and center here. I wouldn't have done it. Not with the gossip train and small-town politics."

"I hear you." He leans forward, elbows on his knees, mason jar dangling from his fingers. "But Happy Cat's more than the gossip and small-town politics."

I try really hard not to roll my eyes—that's *all* I've experienced since getting here ten days ago—but I'm pretty sure I'm failing.

"It is," he insists.

"Maybe for you," I say. Though, honestly, if I weren't presently a virgin attempting to run a sex toy company, I might feel differently about being in the center of a business that inspires so much gossip. I don't need my lack of experience being the next breaking scandal in Happy Cat, and working with sex toys all day makes it all the more likely people will speculate on my love life.

I was more than happy to get out of Happy Cat when I left for college, as much to get out of the

"Savannah Sunshine's older sister" spotlight as anything else. I'm proud of Savannah, but all that attention just isn't for me. Never has been, never will be. The only kind of attention I enjoy is praise from my supervisors, admiration from my peers, and...the way Ryan is looking at me right now, like he'd enjoy dribbling lemonade across my fingertips and sucking off every drop.

God, be still my heart. Seriously—Be. *Still.*

If it pounds any louder, surely Ryan will hear it.

"Not just for me," he insists in this husky voice that makes all the little hairs on the back of my neck lift and my lips feel drunk. Just my lips, which are suddenly hot and kind of numb, but not in a bad way. "You have plans Saturday?"

Plans? What? What is he even talking about with that sexy voice of his? "No," I finally manage to stammer, "b-but I—"

"Great. I'll meet you here at nine."

I blink. "Nine?"

"In the morning," he clarifies with a grin. "So I can show you the glorious secret underbelly of Happy Cat."

I would prefer to see your glorious secret underbelly, I think, but thankfully do *not* say out loud. But I almost do because my lips are under the influence of his sexy voice and his penetrating gaze and the tremendously tremendous smell of him.

"Tremendous," I murmur, eyes going wide as I realize the word escaped my mouth and that, judging by Ryan's grin, he thinks I've just agreed to the underbelly tour. I hurry to backtrack, "I mean, it *would* be tremendous if I didn't have tons of work. Like...tons."

He arches a dubious brow. "On a Saturday morning? When the factory's closed?"

"The sex toy business never sleeps?" I say, but even I know that's weak.

"Savannah misses you, you know," he says. "She talks about you all the time."

I narrow my eyes. "Oh, that's just low."

"Just saying, maybe you'd come see her more often if you knew what you were really missing here." He winks at me, shamelessly, wickedly, and maybe…flirtatiously? "Make sure your bike's ready. We're going to need it."

At that, my cheeks go nuclear again, because I can't think about the bike without thinking about the dildo handlebars and dildos and I still aren't casual acquaintances. "I do enjoy riding bikes, but—"

"I'll pack the lemonade."

He grins again, and I can't help but laugh. "I think you're cheating," I say, swirling the last of the deadly delicious lemonade at the bottom of my mason jar. "This stuff is happy in a glass."

"Good. I'll keep it coming, then. Happy neighbors are important. They throw out fewer things for my raccoon to drag home in the dead of night." He stands. "Nine o'clock Saturday morning. I'll see you here."

I start to hand him back his mason jar, but he shakes his head. "You're not done yet. I'll get it later."

He leaves the house, whistling as he goes, and I wonder what on earth I just agreed to. A friendly outing? A guilt trip from a man who thinks I'm not taking my family obligations as seriously as I should?

Or…a date?

"I think it's a date," I whisper to the bottom of my glass of lemonade, but the lemonade does not respond. Because it's lemonade.

SEVEN

From the town of Happy Cat, Georgia's community InstaChat page.

POST BY Gerald_Hutchins
AKA BakeryBoyHC:

After the nightmare at the Farmer's Market this afternoon, I think we can all agree that it's time for that perverted abomination by the post office to be shut down. PERMANENTLY! How can we call ourselves a town that puts families first when we're harboring something straight out of Jezebel's Closet right in the bosom of our community?

COMMENTS

Tucker87: Ha! He said bosom...

Ruthie_May_Is_Me: Jezebel's Closet! That's a great name for a lingerie store, Gerald. You should open one! Maybe you'd be less cranky if you were surrounded by satin and lace all day.

Emma_June_Jennings: Doubtful. If being up to his elbows in sugar hasn't made him any sweeter, nothing else is going to do the job. Get a life, Gerald! There are children starving in the Sudan, and right here at home for that matter. One in six Georgians are food insecure. Think about that the next time you get your panties in a twist about women seeking pleasure without shame.

Tucker87: You make me insecure, Emma June. How'd you get to be so pretty and so smart?

Emma_June_Jennings: No, Tucker. Just…no. This isn't the time or the place.

Tucker87: Sorry. Are we still on for Saturday night? I'm sorry about what I said at dinner the other night.

Emma_June_Jennings: Not here, Tucker! Text me. And yes. Probably. If you can stay off InstaChat between now and then.

AskAnOldManCarl52: Amen, Gerald! About time someone started talking sense around here. I'm sick of covering my granddaughter's eyes every time I drop a deer head off at the taxidermist's.

Emma_June_Jennings: Oh, so exposing your granddaughter to the DEATH OF A NOBLE CREATURE is no big deal? But God forbid you expose her to a picture of a happy sunshine or the idea that her body and her pleasure both belong to her and neither one is a dirty thing.

AskAnOldManCarl52: She's eight years old!

Emma_June_Jennings: Exactly the right age to start talking about sex! A lot of girls start menstruating at 9 or 10. She's going to be scared to death if someone doesn't talk to her about the facts of life before she wakes up with bloody underwear.

AskAnOldManCarl52: You should be ashamed of yourself, Emma June. Your grandmother raised you better than to talk about your woman time in public.

Emma_June_Jennings: My WOMAN TIME? Are you kidding me right now, dude? Ruthie_May_Is_Me, can you please educate Carl on the way I was raised?

Ruthie_May_Is_Me: Carl, Emma June, both of you need to stop. Nothing was ever solved by fighting on InstaChat. We still on for dinner Sunday, Emma? If so, I'm making pot roast so you might want to bring some of that tofu loaf if you're still not eating meat.

Emma_June_Jennings: I haven't eaten meat in fifteen years, Gran, so yes, I will bring tofu loaf. And wine. Two bottles. I'm going to need them to keep from having a rage stroke every time I get on InstaChat and see how ass-backwards this town is.

AskAnOldManCarl52: I'm not ass-backwards. I'm just tired of feeling uncomfortable, that's all.

Emma_June_Jennings: Then stop, Carl. There's no reason to feel uncomfortable. This is just like the time Bill over at the Feed Store started wearing dresses on Fridays. Everyone was freaked out at first, but we all got used to it. You included. No, it's not business as traditionally usual, but it's fine. And good. And it makes people we care about happy without hurting anyone. How can we complain about that? Honestly.

AskAnOldManCarl52: All right. I'll try. But I'm not talking to Megan about her woman time. That's just taking things too far.

Emma_June_Jennings: Do you want me to talk to her? Since her mama isn't around right now? I don't mind.

AskAnOldManCarl52: Well…yes, I would. Thank you. That's real sweet of you.

Tucker87: Isn't Emma June the sweetest? *kiss emoji* *eggplant emoji* *kiss emoji*

Emma_June_Jennings: Tucker, stop! UGH! Seriously. I'm going to block you from the page if you don't stop embarrassing me.

LetItBurn1234: The fire department should have let that hell hole burn. The longer we tolerate a sex toy factory in the middle of our town, the faster we become a place decent people won't want to call home. That factory gives more jobs to people outside Happy Cat than inside, and attendance at the fish fries and bingo nights is down forty percent. People don't want to be here anymore. How much more money and credibility do we have to lose before the citizens of Happy Cat wake up and smell the rancid lube drying on the face of this once respectable town?

Ruthie_May_Is_Me: I resent this comment. Sunshine is a gift to our community, and brought much-needed economic improvement to a town that's been shrinking since I was a girl. Maybe attendance is down at bingo because it's the same night as the darts tournament at the Wild Hog.

Emma_June_Jennings: And who puts LUBE on their FACE? That's the stupidest thing I've ever heard. Not to mention gross. And the fire department is in the business of saving lives, spooge for brains. There could have been people still inside the factory for all they knew.

LetItBurn1234: There's nothing worth saving in that place, the 'employees' included, and everyone knows it.

Ruthie_May_Is_Me: Oh my Goodness! How awful. Who is this? Gerald is this one of your profiles?

BakeryBoyHC: No, it's not mine. I was trying to stay out of the comments and let everybody else weigh in. But this isn't right. Step back, LetItBurn. I don't like that place any more than you do, but those are good people who work there. Innocent people…even if they do make an indecent number of sex toys.

LetItBurn1234: If those people know what's good for them, they'll start looking for another job. Sooner or later, there's going to be an incident the first responders of Happy Cat aren't prepared to handle and that place is going down. Be a shame if any 'good people' were caught in the crossfire.

BakeryBoyHC: All right, that's enough. This is getting ugly and there's no call for that. We can solve this the democratic way, with a special referendum election to vote on whether or not the factory should be allowed to stay. In the meantime, let's all keep our head on our shoulders and not go off half-cocked.

Tucker87: Heh…you said half-cocked.

Emma_June_Jennings: *heavy sigh* Oh, Tucker…

EIGHT

Ryan

I GET off my forty-eight-hour shift at the fire station at three a.m. Saturday morning and head home to crash for a few hours. Despite the exhaustion making my bones feel hollow—we assisted on three traffic accidents and a fairly serious grease fire during my shift, in addition to fetching George from an industrial garbage bin outside the dollar store, where he was spotted devouring the day old eggs the night manager had thrown out an hour before—I can't sleep.

I'm too keyed up. Too ready for nine o'clock to roll around.

Too excited to see Cassie again, to give her a town tour she's never going to forget, to see her eyes light up when I introduce her to all the good stuff she's been missing in Happy Cat, and to find out if she's going to look at me with that "I want to lick you up and down" gleam in her eye she had Wednesday evening.

If she does, I intend to let her lick me up, down, and any other direction she would care to lick me. And I am fully prepared to return the favor. I want a taste of Cassie's plush mouth the way I want George to start cleaning up his own popcorn mess when he's done watching old episodes of *The Cat Whisperer* on Animal Planet on the couch.

I'm not sure if he's intrigued by the cat whisperer's soothing voice or trying to pick up a few tricks for achieving world domination over the feral cats in our neighborhood, but nothing holds his attention and keeps him out of trouble better. So when he crawls into bed with me a little after four, I turn on the little TV on my bureau and pull up an episode on Hulu.

In just a few minutes, *The Cat Whisperer* has worked his magic on me too, and I'm out like a light.

The next time I open my eyes, it's to the droning of my alarm notifying me that it's eight thirty. I stumble into the shower before I'm fully awake, still drowsy, but determined to get pretty for Cassie. I dry off, run some gel through my hair, and dress in khaki cargo shorts and a tee shirt I dug out of my drawer just for her. I bustle about the kitchen, packing snacks and lunch and putting several bottles of homemade lemonade on ice in my mini cooler, along with a couple of surprises. I load everything into the saddlebags on my bike and push Big Blue over to Cassie's place.

Promptly at nine, I ring her bell. She opens the door so fast, she must have been waiting on the other side, making me smile even before I see her shirt.

"You always wear the most perfect shirts," I say,

nodding toward her *Internet Was Down, So I Thought I'd Go Outside Today* tee shirt.

"Yours isn't bad, either," she says, laughing as she points a finger at my chest where the Sunshine Sex Toy Mascot, Sunny, is getting a big hug from an equally blissed-out looking cat. "Happy Cats Love Sunshine. Was that a gift from Savannah?"

I shake my head. "Nope. I bought one at the gift shop yesterday while we were there on a follow-up visit for the arson investigation. As a show of solidarity. I was hoping I might see you there, but they said you were down at the sheriff's office. Everything all right?"

Her smile droops at the edges. "Some anonymous creep was making veiled threats about doing something to the factory on the town InstaChat page."

"I saw that," I say grimly. "Any progress on figuring out who it was?"

"No. I went to talk to the sheriff about it, but he was at a loss about how to handle a cyber situation. I tried to explain tracking IP addresses to him, but it was like explaining hot air balloons to a fish. And I doubt Insta-Chat would respond to a request from a small-town sheriff for private information on a user anyway. Sheriff Briggs was sympathetic and said he would keep an eye out for suspicious activity, but..."

"But you're not expecting much," I say, wishing I knew something about tracking down cyber trolls. But I'm as clueless as the next guy whose Internet expertise begins and ends with turning his modem on and off in hopes it will fix itself when the signal goes out. All I can do is promise, "Jessie, my chief, and I are keeping a close eye on Sunshine, day and night. We're doing our best to make sure no one gets hurt. And who knows, the lab results might give us a clue who this spooge for brains really is."

Cassie's smile comes out from behind the clouds. "I liked that comment too. Emma June is funnier than I remember. And Tucker even dumber. What does she see in that man?"

I laugh. "Don't quote me, but I'm guessing it has something to do with his face and his muscles. I hear women like those things."

"They do, but I'd rather have a guy who makes me laugh."

"Why not have both?" I tease in a way that makes it pretty damned clear I'm flirting with her. Or trying to anyway. But Cassie only nods calmly and says, "Yeah, that could be good too. Do I need to bring anything? Aside from my wallet and phone?"

"No wallet or phone needed if you don't want them." I step back, motioning toward where my bike is parked at the end of her drive. "I've got everything we need for a day of fun, adventure, and eating all the snacks."

Cassie shuts the door behind her. "I already know I'll like that part of the underbelly tour. Eating all the snacks is one of my favorite things."

"You want to start now?" I ask. "Have you had breakfast?"

She shakes her head. "No, I haven't, but I'm not hungry. I don't do food until after ten o'clock and at least three cups of coffee. I've had two so far."

"Perfect, because we're bound for number three." I head down the walk while she grabs her bike from the far side of the covered porch. "And I'll point out that being able to leave your sweet, dildo-handlebarred bike out all night without locking it up is one of the many benefits to living in a small town."

Cassie laughs. "You're right. In the city, this bad boy would be gone in a heartbeat. I could probably mass produce dildo handlebars and sell thousands of them during Pride Week."

I swing onto my bike. "You should write that down. Get Savannah on the job when she gets back."

"Maybe I will." Cassie mounts her bike beside me, her cheeks going adorably pink as she grips the massive purple dildo handles. "It would be good for her to have something to look forward to, and she loves designing new products. So where are we headed?"

"Somewhere cool," I say mysteriously. "You'll see."

"Okay, but I can't imagine there's anywhere close enough to reach by bike that I haven't seen yet. I've been around Happy Cat a time or two, you know. I did grow up here."

"But you don't know her hidden treasures, Cassie. You haven't taken the time to coax her secrets to the surface."

"So Happy Cat is female?"

"Of course she is. Her name is Happy Cat." I wink before I dart to the left, heading down the trail leading around the lake. "Come on, Sunderwell, look sharp, this coffee isn't going to hunt and kill itself."

TWENTY MINUTES LATER, we're parked outside the Kennedy Family Day School, an abandoned schoolhouse from the late 1800s that's now a general store and sandwich shop that serves the best damned coffee in this or any other county.

Watching Cassie bury her cute little nose in her cup and inhale like she's just sniffed a piece of heaven, it seems she agrees. She takes a cautious sip, her eyes going wide as she swallows. "That is in-fucking-credible." She winces, glancing over her shoulder and laughing in relief when she realizes we're still alone on the front porch rockers. The family of four who ordered breakfast sandwiches behind us are still inside. "Pardon my French, but seriously. How is this so good? What have they done to it?"

"Magic," I say, moaning in appreciation as the smoky, berry, nutty brew goes down as smooth as always. "It's the only explanation."

Cassie lifts her mug to her lips again, eyelashes fluttering with pleasure, making me wonder if that's the face she makes when she experiences other kinds of profoundly pleasurable experiences. I try to put the wayward thought out of my mind, because I'm being a gentleman and a friend first, but then Cassie's dark eyes slit open, meeting mine as her tongue sweeps a sensuous trail across her upper lip, and electricity leaps between us.

"Enjoying your first underbelly tour stop?" I ask, voice husky.

She nods. "I am. I can't believe I didn't know this was here. It's practically in our backyard."

"Now that you're hooked, you'll be making this stop every morning on your way to work."

"I was already thinking about adding a drink holder to the handlebars," she confesses in a whisper, gaze darting guiltily to our bikes in a way that makes me laugh.

"I can probably help you with that. I saw something at the hardware store the other day that would work. I'll get two next time I'm in. One for your bike and one for mine."

Cassie studies me out of the corner of her eyes for a

long beat that makes me wonder if I've said the wrong thing. Before I can ask, her lips curve up in a sweet, almost shy way I've never seen before and she says, "That would be very nice. Thank you."

"You're welcome." The hardware store is now officially on my agenda for this weekend. That smile is too irresistible to wait a single hour longer than necessary to coax it back to her face again. "Want to look at the class photos on the back wall before we go? They've got every year from 1916 to when the school closed in the late seventies."

"Yes!" Her eyes light up. "I love stuff like that. I love seeing how people change so much, but still seem to stay the same, you know?"

I cock my head. "How so?"

"Well, the fashions and the trends are different," she says as we rise, starting back into the store. "But there's always the class clown and the queen bee, the guy everyone falls in love with and the kids too shy to make eye contact with the camera. Still, we all grow up thinking we're the only people who ever got a zit on picture day or were too embarrassed to tell our crush we think they're the bee's knees."

"What does that mean?" I ask. "The bee's knees."

"Fantastic. Excellent. The very best."

I pause with my hand on the screen door. She looks up to find me staring and I smile. "I think you're the bee's knees, Cassandra Sunderwell."

She blushes and I want to kiss her so badly I'm about to go for it, screw taking things slow, when the sandwich family pushes through the door on the other side, instigating a round of apologies from both groups—Cassie and me for blocking the door, them for backing out without looking first.

By the time we get to the back of the store to check out the photos, I figure the moment has passed, but as we're leaning in for a closer look at the class of 1934, Cassie murmurs, "You're pretty bee's knees yourself, O'Dell. But don't let it go to your head."

I grin. "Yes, ma'am."

But it's too late. It's already gone to my head, and my brain is throwing a decidedly premature "Cassie digs us" party.

NINE

Cassie

THIS IS NOT A FRIEND DATE.

This is a *real* date.

I am on a *real* date with Ryan O'Dell, the only person who has ever made me tingle with a glance. And unless I'm absolutely out of my mind, my glances make him tingle too.

I shoot a look his way as we leave our second stop—a covered bridge so quaintly picturesque I've already decided to return with my camera later this week—to find him watching me with a grin on his ridiculously handsome face.

I blush for the hundredth time today as he asks, "Having fun yet?"

"So much fun," I answer honestly, though I shouldn't be. This is dangerous. Letting myself get swept up in the moment with a man like Ryan—a man who doles out sexy stares like candy on Halloween and who is literally ten thousand times more experienced than I am—is a mistake.

Not to mention the fact that he thinks I'm repulsively gross and that kissing me is a breed of torture on par with waterboarding or having his fingernails ripped out with pliers or only getting four chicken wings when he ordered half a dozen.

The thought slows the giddy rush of my heart and makes me wonder, yet again—why are we here? Why this date and the flirting and the sweet offer to set me up with a bike coffee-cup holder of my very own?

Could I be misreading an innocent attempt at friendship?

Or maybe he assumes you've gotten better at locking lips since high school. Ha! As if. He's in for a rude awakening.

I want to tell the inner voice to shut its trap and stop spewing meanness around my brain, but how can I when it's probably right?

I mean, I've had boyfriends—even a couple of serious ones—but I've never made it past third base. I've never been ready and none of my potential partners pushed the issue. And yes, they were all coding nerds, like me, but surely at least one or two should have been so hot for my bod that he was willing to make a play for more than heaving petting.

But they didn't. Not one, not even once.

Until now, I'd assumed that was because they were respectful, sensitive guys who could tell I wasn't ready to take that final step. But as Ryan and I head into the woods, bound for another destination on my dashing companion's oh-so-charming tour, I wonder if maybe teen Ryan was right.

Maybe I am sensually repulsive. Maybe that's why

I'm the oldest virgin in California, the country, and possibly the world.

Maybe I should have taken his words into my head all those years ago, instead of letting them break my heart, and worked hard to suck less at making out.

Though I can't imagine what those steps might have been…

It's not like they offer Foreplay 101 in college and Kissing Classes aren't something you can pick up two-for-one on Groupon. Aside from a steamy practice session with my pillow, I'm not sure I have many options for improving my game.

Unless…

An idea blooms in my head, surging from seed to shade tree in seconds.

I'm so distracted by the mental foliage I don't realize Ryan is slowing down until I'm nearly on top of him. When I do, I shove my heels backward, skidding to an unsteady stop on the leaves in the clearing with a high-pitched yip.

"You okay?" Ryan swings off his bike with the same easy sensuality with which he does all things, this man who has clearly never had to worry about whether he gives good lip lock.

I nod, heart pounding fast, and only partially from the exercise. Can I really do this? Can I open my mouth and make the crazy come out? Can I ask Ryan to be my Tonsil Hockey Tutor?

Um…yes. I think I can.

"No, I'm not okay." I chew my bottom lip for a moment before pulling in a breath and confessing in a rush, "I heard you. What you said. The night we performed our scenes for our parents."

Ryan's brows furrow. "In high school?"

I nod. "Yes. In high school. After we went offstage. When you were behind the curtains?"

"The curtains…" he echoes, looking so confused my cheeks catch fire all over again.

"You know, behind the curtains," I repeat, pulse racing faster as I wonder what the heck I'm going to do if he doesn't remember this almost ten-year-old conversation as well as I do. Probably run off to hide in the forest and perish of starvation and embarrassment. "Before the final bow. When you were chatting with *Ben*," I add, shoulders relaxing away from my ears as his eyes widen and comprehension apparently dawns.

"Oh…with Ben." Ryan nods slowly.

"Yes, with Ben," I say, nodding along with him.

He runs a hand through his hair, making it stick up in an adorable mess on top of his head because everything about this man is adorable. There is literally charisma oozing out of his pores, even when he's uncomfortable. "I'm sorry. I had no idea you were—"

"It's fine, all fine," I hurry to assure him, waving a breezy hand through the air. I don't want to admit to him how badly it hurt. "I mean, it wounded my pride a little as a kid, but that was a long—"

"No, Cassie," he says, shaking his head. "You don't understand. I—"

"Seriously." I force a laugh. "It's no big deal. I wouldn't have brought it up, but there's something I want to ask you, and that conversation is relevant to—"

"No. Listen to me." He leans down, capturing my hands in his as he pins me with a look so intense it steals the rest of my sentence away. Soon, I forget every word I know in English, French, and a smattering of Spanish picked up on a trip to Costa Rica as he adds, "That conversation wasn't about you."

"I'm pretty sure it was," I whisper, pulse disco-dancing in my throat as his fingers curl tighter around mine.

"Okay, yes, it was about you, but not in the way you think. Ben came up to me after our scene to ask me if it was cool to ask you out." Ryan rolls his eyes. "He thought you were 'hot' as Juliet and wanted to make sure there wasn't anything going on between us before he made his move."

My brows lift. "What? But Ben Rathbone hated me."

"He didn't hate you, he was just an asshole who treated girls like shit." Ryan's expression darkens as he adds, "He's still an asshole, by the way. Been divorced three times, and his latest ex had to file a restraining order last week to keep him from setting up his tennis ball launcher in front of her front door and giving her Chihuahua a nervous breakdown with all the pounding."

I huff. "What a jerk."

Ryan nods, lips curving lightly at the edges. "Yeah. He's a bottom feeder. I knew that, even back then, and I couldn't let him get his creepy hands on a sweet kid like you." He shrugs. "So I told him you were a bad kisser."

"I believe the exact words were 'the worst ever' and something about a 'gag-worthy' experience," I say, even as my ribs relax and a light, breezy feeling drifts through my chest.

Could it really be as simple as that?

Just a silly misunderstanding?

All those years of heartache because he was trying to protect me—even if his methods left a lot to be desired.

He winces, his blue eyes wrinkling lightly at the edges. "Yeah, something like that. I'm sorry. You were never supposed to hear any of it. I just couldn't stomach the thought of it—him with you. You looked like you were twelve years old and he was this giant dickhead wrestler."

I cock my head, torn between being touched and troubled. I want to believe him, but I still remember how badly it hurt. And I don't ever want to feel that way again. "But I wasn't twelve years old, Ryan. I was sixteen, and as capable of telling Ben to get lost as you were. It wasn't your place to make decisions for me like that. Especially not by spreading a story that I kissed like the creature from the black lagoon."

"You're right. And I'm sorry. I guess..." He trails off with an uncomfortable shrug. "I couldn't help myself, I guess. I was so used to getting between my brothers and trouble, my gut instinct was to do whatever it took to make sure the people I cared about stayed out of trouble."

The lightness in my chest transforms into a warm, pleasantly fierce ache. "So you...cared about me?"

Ryan nods, his fingers threading through mine, making me keenly aware of the fact that we're still touching and that he's making no move to let me go. "I did. You were so smart and funny. You made me laugh more than anyone I'd ever met, and...I liked you. Probably liked you too much considering how much older I was."

I laugh, soft and breathy. "You were only two years older."

"I had over a foot on you, Sunderwell. You were even more of a wee thing back then."

"A wee thing?" I tilt my head back, lips buzzing as he shifts closer. "You really should know better than to insult a person's size. We short people are notoriously crazy when we're angry. Just look at Napoleon. Genghis Khan. Tom Cruise."

He grins, a big, beautiful O'Dell-special that zings

straight from my heart to my panties and back again, making me feel like a sparkler on the Fourth of July. "Genghis Khan, huh? Sounds like I should be scared."

"Terrified," I murmur as his head dips closer to my upturned face.

It's the perfect word. I *am* terrified.

But I'm also filled with a million fizzy bubbles of anticipation. And then Ryan's lips cover mine and the bubbles dump into my bloodstream, hitting faster than a shot of tequila on an empty stomach. His tongue traces the seam of my mouth as his arms go around my waist and then my hands are tangled in his hair and he's dragging me close and we're kissing in a way I've never kissed anyone in my life—hard, deep, and oh-so-breathless.

My nipples pull tight in my sports bra and visions of baseball diamonds dance behind my closed eyes.

Suddenly, I can imagine running all four of those bases with this man. With Ryan, Patron Saint of Kissing and Captain of my Panties.

"Oh captain, my captain," I whisper when we finally come up for air.

"*Dead Poets Society?*" Ryan murmurs, sounding as breathless as I feel.

"Walt Whitman," I say. "I've never seen *Dead Poets Society*."

Ryan's eyes narrow as he clucks his tongue disapprovingly. "Never? It's a modern classic."

I shake my head. "Never."

"Then we'll have to fix that tonight. My place. Popcorn and a movie at seven sharp."

I grin, both because he's not running for cover after *this* kiss, and because my heart's leaping all over the place. He wants to extend our date! The heart discoing might actually be mutual. "Okay. I think I can fit you into my busy schedule."

He arches a brow, his fingertips digging into my hips as he says, "That's nice of you."

"I'm a nice person," I say, tingling all over again as his mouth moves back within devouring distance.

"You are. So nice." His lips move against mine as he speaks the last two words, making me pretty sure he isn't talking about my high moral fiber.

He's talking about this kiss, *my* kiss.

Looks like I might not need make-out lessons after all.

TEN

Ryan

WE STAY out for the rest of the day—biking secret trails through the forest, picnicking in an abandoned tree house my brothers and I fixed up last summer, zip-lining at Canopy Tours over by the lake, and getting a second cup of coffee and a cinnamon bun to share at the Kennedy school before heading for home.

And even though I know I'm probably coming on too strong, I can't resist parking my bike in the drive next to hers and taking her hand before she can say goodbye. "Want to come over now? I can whip up some dinner before we do movie and popcorn."

"Or we could just have popcorn for dinner," Cassie says, making my heart do that fist pump thing it does when she looks at me in that new, unguarded way that makes it clear things are good between us.

Hell, things are *great* between us. I can't remember the last time I had this much fun and that kiss….

Fuck, that kiss…

She is so delicious, so sexy I could have spent the entire day making out with her in the middle of nowhere. As long as I had Cassie, soft and curvy in my arms, I wouldn't have felt like I was missing out on a damned thing.

And now she's coming over to my place, letting me hold her hand as I lead her inside and shut the door. Now, I have an entire evening with her, too. It might be silly, but I feel like I've won the lottery. As I get out the popcorn pan and kernels, I'm flying so high I don't notice that George hasn't toddled in to welcome me home until Cassie asks where he is.

"I don't know." I glance into the living room from my place by the stove only to find George's usual napping spot in the corner of the couch empty. "He might have let himself out through the cat door to use the facilities. He'll be back once he hears the popcorn popping. He's addicted to the stuff."

Cassie laughs. "Really? Can he eat that? Is that okay?"

"Totally fine. I asked the vet. As long as it doesn't have any butter or salt on it."

"But we're going to have butter and salt on ours, right?" she asks hopefully.

"Hell, yes, we are," I say, laughing as she claps her hands happily.

"Excellent. But don't worry, I won't tell George."

"That's good of you. Don't want him to know you're getting special treatment." I wink at her, loving the way she flushes in response.

But it turns out we don't have to worry about

George's butter-induced jealousy. He doesn't show up for movie time and Cassie and I have the entire couch to ourselves. We snuggle close, her tucked under my arm with no cuddle bandit wedged in between us with popcorn strewn across his furry belly. It's nice, more than nice, and by the time the credits roll, Cassie is practically in my lap, our empty popcorn bowls discarded on the floor by the couch so we could get as close as two people can get while upright and fully clothed.

"That was sad." Cassie sniffs as she lifts her shimmering eyes to mine. "But lovely."

"You're lovely," I say, tucking a lock of silky soft hair behind her ear.

Her eyes tighten around the edges. "No, I'm not. I'm cute. On a good day."

"No, you're beautiful. Every day." I kiss her again, proving the fireworks earlier today weren't a freak occurrence. They're just what happen when our lips meet, when she sighs into my mouth and her tongue dances with mine and her breasts flatten against my chest, threatening to give me a heart attack.

I can't remember the last time I wanted a woman this much, if I've *ever* wanted a woman this much.

"Ryan, I need to tell you something," Cassie says as I urge her thighs to either side of my hips.

"Yeah?"

She straddles me, the seam of her shorts pressing against where I'm already hard, and I fight a groan. Her breath hitches as I slip my hand beneath the hem of her shirt.

"Um…nothing. It's nothing," she says.

"Are you sure?" I cup her breast through her spandex bra, head spinning as she arches into my touch, silently giving me permission to keep doing what I'm doing.

"Yes," she whispers, then, "Oh, yes," shivering as I brush my thumb over the tight peak straining the thin fabric.

"I want to see you, Cassie." I capture her nipple between my finger and thumb, rolling gently. "I want to kiss you everywhere."

She nods and reaches for the bottom of her shirt in response. I help her whip her clothes over her head—first her tee shirt, then her bra—and in mere moments I'm cupping her breasts reverently in both hands. She's stunning, so breathtaking it takes a beat for my tongue to remember how to make words and then a beat longer to decide words are a waste at a time like this.

I lean in, kissing first one dusky pink tip and then the other, circling the taut flesh with my tongue before sucking her gently into my mouth.

"Oh my God, Ryan." Cassie's fingers thread into my hair, pulling me close as her head falls back. "Oh my God."

I groan against her softness and suckle her deeper as she grinds against me, every roll of her hips making me hotter, harder, until I can barely breathe, barely think. There is nothing in my head but Cassie—her salt and flower scent, the sexy sounds she makes as I transfer my attention to her other perfect breast, the way her arms tremble on either side of my face as she digs her fingernails into the skin at the back of my neck and her breath comes faster.

I'm about to ask if I can carry her down the hall—to my bedroom, to *my bed*, where I intend to show her just how good my tongue can make other parts of her feel—when it happens.

One second I'm kissing Cassie's incomparable breasts while she rides me through our clothes, and the next a large, heavy, Unidentified Falling Object plops down between us with a high-pitched squeal.

Suddenly, my mouth is full of fur and chaos is breaking out on the couch.

Cassie screams, I grunt, and the psychotic fur ball wedged between us chitters in panic, raking his claws down my throat and trying to get off my lap by going through my face. Cassie cries out again and scrambles off my lap and I'm left with a fat-ass, mood-killing raccoon curled around my shoulders like a mink stole.

George's tail is in my mouth, and both of his clawed hands cover my eyes, obstructing the view of Cassie grabbing her clothes from the floor.

By the time I coax the furry beast off my head and off the couch, Cassie's shirt is back on and she's dashing across the living room.

"I'm sorry," I say, standing up fast. "I don't know what got into him. He must have fallen asleep up there and then decided he was ready to get down the fast way."

"On the fan?" Cassie says with a tight laugh.

"He did it once before. No idea how he gets up there." I shoot George a hard look as he winds around my leg and sits down on my foot, impeding my progress toward Cassie with his stubborn bulk. "But I'll figure it out. Please, don't go."

"I have to," she says, motioning toward the front door as she continues to back away. "I have a thing. Work thing. In the morning. I should go and get some sleep. But thank you. For today. It was wonderful."

"It was. But are you sure you have to go? It's not even eight o'clock."

"Yeah. Busy day tomorrow," she says, grabbing her keys off the entry table. "Lots of things to lube." She winces. "I mean to do. Sorry, I have to go. Now." With a frantic wave and a promise to "call soon" tossed over her shoulder, she slams out my front door into the night, leaving me with a hard-on for her that won't quit and a cock-blocking raccoon grinning up at me in a way that makes it obvious he has no shame.

None. At all.

ELEVEN

From the texts of Cassie Sunderwell and Savannah Sunderwell

Cassie: I have a problem.

Savannah: Crap, I totally forgot to mention that the coffeemaker has its own water supply. So sorry! I thought you knew. Don't worry about the mess. Text Tina and tell her to charge the cleanup to my account. She should be there sometime next week for the normal monthly cleaning too.

Cassie: No, not with the coffeemaker. I'm proficient in coffeemaker. ALL coffeemakers.

Savannah: Phew. Good. I know how much you love your coffee. Oh, no, I mentioned the rocks, but I think I forgot to mention George Cooney too. Did he sneak in the window and steal your pajamas? That little cutie is a sucker for silk, which is only awkward when he tries to wear it. Not that he shouldn't be free to explore his own fashion sense and sexuality, but we're nowhere near the same size.

Cassie: Um, not George. Exactly. I mean, George is fine. In an annoying kind of way, but he's…yeah.

Savannah: Please don't tell me it's Olivia. Her chart readings always get dark around the new moon phase. Whatever she said, I promise it's not that bad.

Cassie: Aww, listen to you! You miss Happy Cat, don't you?

Savannah: No. Yes. Maybe. I mean, I miss the people. The people who aren't lying cheating sheep-lovers. *sheep emoji* *broken heart emoji* *knife emoji* And I miss the blissful ignorance of not knowing I was married to one. And that time before people thought I would lie about a man compromising a sheep. But I've discovered I love tea time and scones. And being in a place where people don't recognize me. And sleeping in until eight.

Cassie: Eight at NIGHT?

Savannah: No, silly. Eight in the morning. Who sleeps until eight at night?

Cassie: Who thinks sleeping until eight in the morning is SLEEPING IN?

Savannah: LOL – you're such a night owl. I love that

about you. And I miss you most. You're the sun in my sunshine. *sun emoji*

Cassie: I miss you too. You're the mega in my byte. *binary emoji*

Savannah: Okay, my little dove. Tell me about this problem so I can be a useful sister. Do you need advice on what size dildo to grab?

Cassie: No. I have a real life penis problem. Ryan O'Dell kissed me. And then some. But not…all the way.

Savannah: Oh, honey. I'm so sorry. *barf emoji*

Cassie: It wasn't barfy at all. It was pretty amazing, actually. If I hadn't freaked out when George fell off the ceiling fan, I probably wouldn't be a virgin anymore, which is weirdly scary. But exciting. But also scary! Because what the hell is going on with my life all of a sudden? With the fancy coffee and the romantic bike rides and the zip-lining and the "you're beautiful every day" stuff? I swear, I am so confused right now.

Savannah: I don't understand half of that, but I'm buying George all the candy and broken dildos in the world to thank him.

Cassie: WHAT? Why? I thought you WANTED me to experience sexual pleasure, not to get cockblocked by a trash panda!

Savannah: Oh, honey, I do. I do! But not with RYAN.

Cassie: I know, I hated him in high school after Romeo-and-Juliet-Gate, but that was a big misunderstanding. We've both grown up a lot since then, and he was so sweet when he took me on a tour of town this morning. And he thinks I'm funny and I have so much fun with him and then he kissed me, and I liked it. And then we went a little further, and I liked it more, and then… Raccoonus Interruptus.

Savannah: No! Oh, Cassie, just no. No kissing. PLEASE DO NOT KISS RYAN AGAIN.

Cassie: Why? OMG. He has a girlfriend, doesn't he? And I'm the last one to know. Of course. Or—OMG, does he secretly like sheep too?

Savannah: Cassie. He's a MAN. With a PENIS. *angry profanity emoji* *eggplant emoji* *knife emoji*

Cassie: Well, yes. I noticed. I REALLY noticed, believe me. But does he have a girlfriend? Or some creepy, top-secret fetish I should know about?

Savannah: Penises – peni? – are BAD.

Cassie: So no girlfriend? Or sheep friend? Other farm animal friend? Please tell me that he and George are just pals. PLEASE. Or I won't be able to sleep tonight.

Savannah: Ryan O'Dell is a normal, healthy, kind, smart, caring, responsible person who had the unfortunate luck to have been born a male of the species, a condition for which there is currently no cure. So please, dearest sister, PLEASE get thee to a dildo. Dildos can't hurt you. I mean, maybe if you forget the lube and aren't in the mood, they might, but they're not going to savage your soul with their betrayal. The dildos still want to help. And they won't get jealous if you throw a vibrator into the mix. Which, by the way, I also have a stash of unopened vibrators in the bottom drawer in the vanity. Help yourself to those too.

Cassie: So to clarify, your objection is ONLY that he's a man, and not that you have evidence that he's a BAD man?

Savannah: If you HAD to choose a man, you couldn't choose a better one. However, you DON'T have to choose a man. You can choose to embrace the power to provide your own happiness, satisfaction, and orgasms. You have to love yourself first and most, Cassie. If you love someone else first or most, you'll lose yourself. And then you'll find yourself twenty pounds later after a torrid love affair with English tea and scones and wonder if you'll ever fit back into a size eight. But you can love yourself WITHOUT ever having to go through all that pain, suffering, and scone-induced hip-spreading.

Cassie: I'm not asking him to marry me, Van. He's a wild stallion. I'm a sea cow who's blind in one eye. I'm just considering letting him kiss me again because I actually liked it. I'm smart enough not to let emotions get involved.

Savannah: Oh, pumpkin pie. YOU ARE THE STALLION. He's barely a sea cucumber. And at least promise me he's putting his fair share of effort into the kissing.

Kissing *is* nice. And so far, there's no artificial substitute. *frowny face emoji*

Cassie: You could work on that if you came home. Sunshine Toys could develop a lip dildo that simulates kissing. OMG, I just typed that.

Savannah: You should come here, instead. There's no reason to keep trying to salvage Sunshine Toys when you could be here with me in Europe where the people are wonderful and the food is full of delicious butter and the roundabouts are so adorable and efficient.

Cassie: The roundabouts? Savannah. You're praising ROUNDABOUTS. What's going on? Are you okay?

Savannah: Olivia should come too. We could buy an old English estate and turn it into a haven for women who have been done wrong in the game of love. We'll serve tea all hours of the day and teach women that their sexual satisfaction is important, and that their emotional and spiritual well-being is paramount.

Cassie: I don't have the training for any of that. And you don't have to start over in England! You have half of everything you're talking about right here, in Happy Cat! Sunshine Toys is just the start. When you get back, you can add extra staff for website expansion with a blog and life enrichment courses. Also, the deserted Mason plantation near the county line would be perfect for retreats. You could renovate it and bring English tea time to Georgia! The driveway is so long, you could even have a roundabout.

Savannah: You are such a sweet, sweet optimist, dear Cassie.

Cassie: I learned it from you, Savannah. I miss you. Olivia misses you. Ruthie May misses you. The Happy Cat Gazette misses you. Olivia's been writing your weekly column, but the last one was a sex position chart based on astrological sign that was four thousand words too long. The editor chucked it and ran a column on making homemade donuts instead, and now everyone's arguing over yeast versus cake instead of getting in touch with their sexuality.

Savannah: No one wants my advice right now.

Cassie: I do! I want your advice.

Savannah: No. I can't endorse healthy sexual relationships because I don't know what they look like. I'm a fraud. And it's high time I figure out what else I can do with my life.

Cassie: Getting hurt because you loved someone does not make you a fraud. It makes you human and real and even wiser than you were before. The women of the world need you, Savannah. And everyone in Happy Cat misses you and supports you.

Savannah: Not Gerald and all those people who think I'm lying about Steve's torrid love affair with a sheep.

Cassie: Gerald misses you too! He told me so just yesterday.

Savannah: He misses me buying cinnamon rolls for staff meetings every Monday morning. By the way, you should buy cinnamon rolls for the staff meeting Monday morning.

Cassie: The staff miss you too. And forget those people who don't believe you. They'd take sides with a toaster just to be obstinate.

Savannah: I can't come home, Cassie. Not yet. I'm meant to be here. I can feel it. I just don't know why yet.

Cassie: Well… If I can help you figure it out, you know I'm here.

Savannah: I love you, sissy.

Cassie: I love you too, pumpkin.

Savannah: Now quit kissing men and go dig into the secret drawer. *heart emoji* *hug emoji* *eggplant emoji*

TWELVE

Ryan

IT'S TEN, Cassie's normal breakfast time, and I have a stack of waffles with her name on it. I don't know if waffles are a good *I'm sorry my raccoon fell on us while we were making out* offering, but if they don't work, I have a few more tricks up my sleeve.

I'm pulling the heated stack out of the oven when my phone rings.

Ruthie May's calling.

I brace myself. It's Sunday morning, and most of the gossip about Jace and Ginger comes in on Sundays. Saturday is Ginger's favorite night to hang out at the Wild Hog.

I want to see Cassie, but if my brother's in a bad spot, I'll be there.

I put the waffles back in the oven and swipe to answer. "Mornin', Ruthie May."

"Ryan. Are you home? Have you looked at InstaChat this morning? Is the sheriff headed down your street?"

My pulse leaps and I start for the door, grabbing my keys on the way. "What happened? Where's Jace? Is he okay?"

"Jace? You think Jace had something to do with it?" She cackles. It's a muffled cackle, like she's trying to hide it, but it still carries through the line. "Oh, you think he found Ginger's stash?"

"Stash?" *Fuck*. She's into drugs? If she's getting my brother hooked, I will kill her. Never pegged her for the druggie type, but I've been wrong a time or two. "Stash of *what*?"

"Of sex toys," Ruthie May says. "Jealousy makes a man do crazy things."

My pulse starts to slow as I drop my keys back on their hook. "Ruthie May, what the *hell* are you talking about?"

"You haven't been online today? Or seen Cassie?"

"Cassie? No. Not y—Ruthie May. Spell this out for me."

I grab my tablet and pull up InstaChat, which Ruthie May probably suspects I'm doing, because instead of going for a dramatic delivery, she blurts, "The dildo-pocalypse hit Main Street last night!"

I open my mouth to answer, but my screen is suddenly filled with pictures of sex toys littered all over Main Street and Sunshine Square, named after the *Savannah Sunshine* TV show, of course, not the sex toy factory.

Dildos in all shapes, sizes, and colors. Feather ticklers. Vibrators. Condoms. Packets of lube. Some stuff that I can't even identify, but which sort of resembles gymnastic equipment.

"Are you looking at the pictures?" Ruthie May is breathless with excitement.

"Uh-huh," I confirm.

"You think Jace did it?"

"What—*no*. I thought he— Ruthie May, I can promise you with utmost certainty that neither I nor any of my brothers had anything to do with this. I'm ending this conversation now."

"Okay, but can you go check on Cassie? You were about to say you hadn't seen her *yet*, weren't you? You two have plans?"

An incoming call beeps through. I glance at my phone display and can't help a grin.

There's something magical about Cassie's name lighting up my phone. There's also relief that she's still willing to talk to me.

"No, Ruthie May. I have to go so I can go feed George his breakfast."

"He's out in the square gnawing on a dildo right now."

Shit. My phone beeps again. "Good to know. Talk to you later, Ruthie May." I hang up and switch over to Cassie's call. "Hey, pretty neighbor. You doin' okay?"

"Ah, um…" she replies, her voice strained.

"Listen, don't sweat it. The sheriff will figure out—"

"*No*! No, please don't call the sheriff."

"Cassie?"

"It took me twenty minutes just to work up the nerve to call you. *Promise* me you won't call the sheriff."

"Okay, okay. No sheriff. I'm coming over, and we'll figure this out, okay?"

"Can you—could you—leave your phone at home?" she whispers.

"I—"

"*Please?*"

"Okay."

"Just let yourself in. The door's open. Bye."

She hangs up before I can ask anything else. I hesitate long enough to grab the hot plate of waffles, then I dash out the door and across our lawns. When I get to Savannah's house, I duck under the *Steve The Cheater Doesn't Live Here Anymore* sign, give a quick knock, then push the door open. "Cassie?"

"Are you alone?" comes the muffled answer from somewhere near the back of the house.

"All alone," I confirm, setting the plate on the coffee table in the living room before pushing farther into the cottage. "You okay?"

There's a pause. "Mostly."

I follow her voice. "Where are you?"

"The bathroom."

There's a wince in her voice that sends me speeding through the living room and down the hall to Savannah's bedroom, which is almost as Zen-like as I would've imagined it. Warm colors on the walls, paper lantern lampshades, and the soft scent of something I can't identify tickles my nose. "Cassie?"

"You left your phone at home?" Her voice echoes from a doorway around the other side of the king-size bed with the white fluffy comforter that's wrinkled in the middle of the mattress. Despite my best intentions, I can't tamp down the primal surge of arousal that ricochets through me at the thought of Cassie tangled up in that bed.

"Phone's at home. What's wrong?"

"Just—" There's a huge sigh. "This is so freaking embarrassing," she mutters.

"Can I come in?" I ask, hesitating by the door to the open bathroom.

"Yes," she moans.

Slowly, I step inside and for the second time in five minutes, I'm speechless.

She's covering her face with her hands, but her cheeks and neck are scarlet, flaming red. Even her arms are blushing.

So are her bare legs.

Which are sticking out of the toilet all akimbo, her toes at attention in the air.

She's *stuck* in the toilet, the poor thing. The room is so large, she can't touch her hands or her legs to the walls except maybe the wall behind her, and the toilet is one of those insanely tall models.

"My ass is trapped," she says without taking her hands off her face. One eye is completely blocked by her cell phone, which has a cover featuring a cartoon Viking sticking a flag in a planet. "I've fallen into the bowl and I can't get out."

I fight a laugh. "Hazard of having such a petite backside, I suppose."

She groans beneath her breath. "Can you *not* look at me while you pull me out? And then go home and pretend this never happened? I need one of those flashy memory-wiping thingies from *Men in Black*. Where's the app for that?"

I cock my head, studying the situation, figuring I should be able to lift her out by her armpits. "Consider my memory wiped," I assure her. "I'm going to grab you around the ribs and pull, okay?"

"With your eyes closed and no cameras and no judging my grossness?"

My chest aches. "Cassie," I say gently. "Hey. Look at me."

She parts her fingers and peers through the cracks at

me with one eye. Her cell phone is still covering the other. I don't ask how she managed to hold onto her phone while falling into the toilet—it's both irrelevant and understandable.

Who among us has not played Candy Crush while using the facilities?

"No one's taking any pictures you don't want taken," I promise. "Not on my watch. And I won't breathe a word about this to anyone. Promise. You're safe with me."

She stares at me without blinking for three long heartbeats, long enough for me to feel the weight of the realization that I *can't* always keep her safe, or protect her every minute of the day.

But I can shield her from Mortification By Toilet.

"Thank you," she whispers.

I take that as permission, close my eyes, wrap my arms around her warm tee shirt, and tug.

She makes a *glerg* noise, and I realize her legs are stuck pretty good.

"I have a defective bottom," she grumbles. "I should change my name to Cassie Weirdbottom."

I smile, but keep my eyes closed. "It's not you. It's the toilet. Where did Savannah get this thing?"

"Torture Toilets R-Us?" she guesses.

I stop myself from laughing, only because I don't want her to think I'm laughing *at* her instead of *with* her. "Didn't realize there was a market for those."

She lets out a soft laugh, and that organ in my chest melts. I want to make her laugh like that every day. All the time.

But first I have to get her out of this toilet. I tug again, she yips and squeezes me tight, but she's still not budging.

Her arms are twined around my neck, though, that

fresh scent of salty flowers tickles my nose, and her breath is hot on my shoulder as she whispers, "Ryan?"

"Yeah?"

"While I'm already mortified, I have to tell you something."

THIRTEEN

Cassie

RYAN STARTS TO PULL BACK, but I grip him tighter. I'm already embarrassed, and I don't want to see his reaction.

I also don't want to chicken out.

"I'm a virgin," I blurt out.

His whole body goes as stiff as—well, as stiff as that part of him that was between my legs last night. Which I wouldn't mind feeling again, because *wow*—how electric was that? And intense? And so all-over-buzzy-and-tingly that I finally get it.

I get why people like sex so much.

They like it because it feels so incredible, so close, intimate in a way nothing else ever has. It felt like I was touching something deeper than Ryan's warm skin or rock hard muscles. Like my heartbeat and his were pounding in time, playing a song only the two of us could hear.

A beautiful song, so much sweeter than I imagined something sexual could ever be.

But sadly, this is not the time for romance.

He's attempting to pull me out of a *toilet*. And going completely silent. And whatever sexy points I might have racked up yesterday, I have probably now ruined.

He disentangles himself and pulls back to look at me, his brows pinched while he squats to my level. I can't tell if he's disappointed or appalled or shocked or all of the above.

Also, my legs are going numb.

"Cassie." He touches gentle fingers to my cheek. "You don't have to be embarrassed."

"Mortified is the word of the day," I whisper.

He doesn't blink.

I clear my throat. "Right. Maybe not if you're a normal, everyday, socially inept geek who *isn't running a sex toy company*. But…"

He doesn't laugh.

Nope. His eyes go dark and his Adam's apple bobs and he glances down quickly before meeting my gaze again. "So you really…never?"

His voice is husky too, and even though I'm being eaten alive by a toilet, the sparks radiating between us are heating my skin, making it hard to breathe.

"Never," I confirm, my lips continuing to flap, spilling all my secrets. "I've never even had a close encounter with a dildo. Van keeps suggesting I help myself, but I just…I'm not…" I exhale with a sharp huff. "And now I need to get out of this toilet and get downtown to help clean up the mess someone's made, which means I'll have to juggle dildos like I'm a pro. But I'm just *not*, and—"

He puts his fingers to my lips. "I'll get you some gloves. And I'll get my brothers. We'll all help."

"*No!* With your brothers and half the town watching, I'll be even more embarrassed."

His smile is growing. "I just realized, we missed part of our tour yesterday."

"The part where there are sex toys everywhere and someone's clearly using dildo graffiti to get more people on board with shutting down Sunshine Toys?"

"The part where, no matter how strange the circumstances, everyone pitches in to help during a crisis."

"Everyone is *not* pitching in."

"They are. C'mon. Let's get you out of here, I'll grab reinforcements, and we'll meet you downtown for Operation Toy Clean-up."

He leans down, looping his arms around me again. "We're just gonna wiggle until we get it, okay?"

"That's not how I hear it works," I grumble.

He laughs, and I can't help smiling back.

Because even though this is embarrassing, having Ryan here is all the reassurance I need that everything is going to be okay.

FOURTEEN

Ryan

TURNING off the highway onto the gravel drive to Jace's place, I force myself to keep my speed to a respectable thirty miles per hour. It hasn't rained in over a week and I don't want to coat Blake's grape crop with dust.

My second to youngest brother is serious about starting a small vineyard in the next four years and has given each of us the "respect the fruit, assholes" lecture more times than I can count. He's usually the most laid back of the four of us, but mess with his latest Big Plan and you'll see a side of Blake that isn't sunshine and rainbows.

But it's hard to go slow, and not just because I'm past ready to be back with Cassie, helping her make downtown a sex toy-free zone while acquiring further information about how this whole "still a virgin" situation came to pass.

She's a gorgeous, funny, sexy, intelligent woman who's a blast to spend time with.

And sexy.

Have I mentioned sexy? Or that she kisses like a house on fire, which is something I know about from firsthand experience. It's intense, awe-inspiring, scary and magnificent all at once.

Like Cassie Sunderwell, though it's clear she has no idea how irresistible she is.

But even though she's pretty much the only thing running through my head, I can't fight the gut feeling that something's wrong with Jace.

My brothers all joke about my "Big Bro-Dar," but in all the years I've been keeping them out of trouble, it's never steered me wrong. First, my shoulders get restless, then my stomach starts to ache, and before long I can't stop pacing until I get whatever sibling is plaguing my thoughts on the phone.

Or, better yet, corner the kid in question in person.

Though, of course, they aren't kids anymore. Hell, they haven't been for a long time. *I* haven't been a kid since I was ten, the day we almost lost my youngest brother, Clint, when he ran outside to play in the rain and ended up getting struck by lightning. I was supposed to be watching him.

He almost died because I hadn't kept him inside.

From that day forward, I'd made it my mission to keep my brothers safe and to never, ever do anything to hurt them again.

Clint now credits his near-death experience for his dauntless, rise-to-the-challenge attitude that's made him the most decorated young marine in his unit.

Which is fine and all—I'm proud of Clint, I really am

—but I would rather keep the people I care about out of harm's way.

As if summoned by my danger-avoiding thoughts, a red Jetta appears at the end of the road in front of me. Long before the car gets close enough to get a good look at the driver, I know who it is.

There's only one red Jetta in Jace's life, and it's driven by his heart-breaker of an on-again-off-again girlfriend, Ginger.

I slow down even more, forcing myself to nod civilly to the redhead behind the wheel as our vehicles pass each other on the road. For her part, Ginger is smirking as she wiggles scarlet-tipped nails behind her closed window. She looks pretty satisfied with herself, which can only mean one thing—she and Jace are back together.

"Shit," I curse, my heart sinking. For a moment, I consider heading back to town without collecting Jace or Blake for help with clean-up—I'm clearly too late to pull my brother out of harm's way —but I keep going. Cassie really could use the help and my Big-Bro-Dar is still blaring out a code red.

It doesn't take long to realize why.

I reach the circle drive in front of Jace's split-level ranch to find him sitting on the porch swing, his head buried in his hands, and his dark hair sticking up in a dozen different directions. The slump to his shoulders signals that this is bad, even worse than the time Ginger allegedly played beer pong with Bart Tompkins, only with golf balls. And her cleavage.

"What's up, brother?" I slam out of the door, scanning the porch and the vegetable garden beyond. "Blake around? He said he was going to be out here this morning."

"He's around somewhere, but you're not here to see

Blake," Jace says, followed by a heavy sigh so tortured the worry twisting in my gut ratchets up another notch. "Your tail was tingling again, wasn't it?"

"Maybe." I climb the four stairs to the porch. "What's up? I passed Ginger on my way up the drive."

He lifts his head, pinning me with a hard look. "You didn't flip her off again, did you?"

"I didn't flip her off last time," I say, rolling my eyes. "I was adjusting my visor. The sun was in my eyes."

"Adjusting your visor with your middle finger stuck out?"

"I don't know. Maybe. I don't remember, which is why I apologized to Ginger for the misunderstanding." I stop in front of him, leaning back against the porch railing. "You know me better than that, Jace. I believe in minding my manners, even with people whose behavior, in my opinion, isn't always up to snuff."

"My opinion either," he says, surprising me. "Which is why I told Ginger it was over. For good."

My jaw drops, but I snap it closed again before he can see my reaction.

"Wow." I nod, fighting to keep my enthusiasm to a minimum. Jace and Ginger have been a couple for a long time. This can't have been easy for him, no matter how sick he is of her head games. "So…how'd she take it? She looked all right."

She looked weirdly happy, in fact, a condition that makes more sense when Jace says, "She took it just fine. We were back together again two minutes later so there wasn't much time to get upset."

I fight the urge to curse aloud. "Oh. Well then…"

"Yeah, I know." Jace pushes to his feet, pacing restlessly away across the porch. "But it isn't like all the other times, Ryan. I was going to go through with it. I was fucking done, I swear, and it felt so good."

I shake my head. "So what happened?"

He turns to face me, his eyes tightening around the edges. "She's pregnant."

This time I can't hold back the curse, or the question I know I shouldn't ask. "Are you sure it's yours?"

"Yes, I'm sure, asshole," he says, his temper flaring. "She's exactly two months along and you know where we were two months ago."

I press my lips together. "In Mexico. At the beach."

"At a deserted beach," he adds, "without another soul in sight. For ten days. There's no way that baby isn't mine."

I exhale slowly. "So it's yours. That doesn't mean you and Ginger have to be a couple. Lots of people raise kids together, but separately."

His features stiffen and a familiar stubbornness flickers to life in his eyes. "Yeah, I know. But despite what the rest of you think, the black sheep of the family has a moral code, too, you know."

"I never said you didn't. And you're not the black—"

"And I'm not about to bail on being there for my kid just because it hasn't always been smooth sailing with Ginger," he barrels on. "I don't want to be an every other weekend parent. I want to be there full-time, every day, every night. I don't want to be a stranger in my own baby's life."

Chest aching with a mixture of empathy and pride, I nod. "I get it. Point taken. And for what it's worth, I think you're going to be a great father."

Jace crosses his arms and rolls his eyes. "Right. Sure you do. Don't lay it on too thick there, bro."

"I'm not laying it on thick." I rest a hand on his shoulder, waiting until he grudgingly meets my gaze before I say, "Seriously. You've got this. You work hard, you've got a good heart, and you're a lot of fun when you're not being a cranky bastard."

His lips quirk. "Yeah, well…I'm working on that too. I told Ginger we have to go to therapy. Get a handle on our shit before the baby comes."

My eyebrows shoot up so fast for a second I think I've popped a contact. And I don't even wear contacts.

He laughs in response. "You should see your face. I wish I had a picture to show you the next time you tell me you're good at poker."

"I'm incredible at poker."

My brother smirks. "And I'm the King of France."

"Fine. You're on. As soon as Dad and Mom get back from their cruise, it's family poker night, my house. I'll make the queso dip and you can bring a jar full of nickels for me to take off your hands."

"I'm in," Blake announces from behind me.

I turn to see my second to youngest brother—the only one of us with Mom's green eyes—bounding up the porch steps, his white tee shirt and battered brown Carhartt work pants streaked with dirt. "I've been jonesing for a poker night." He shoves a hand through his sun-streaked brown hair, which is past his shoulders and nearly as long as our mother's too, and squints Jace's way. "What's up? You okay? I saw Ginger head out."

"Jace can fill you in on the way." I jab a thumb toward my truck. "I need your help. A dildo bomb exploded in downtown. I told Cassie we'd come help with clean-up."

Blake's lips curve into a shit-eating grin. "Cassie Sunderwell, huh? I heard you were out with her yesterday. Didn't she used to hate you in high school?"

"Like it was her job," Jace agrees, nudging me in the ribs. "But you know Ryan. Never met a woman he couldn't smolder into a puddle at his feet."

"I'm not smoldering at anyone," I say, though I'll admit a part of me likes the idea of Cassie in lust-puddle form because of my smoldering skills.

The other part of me, however, is still stuck on the Big Reveal.

I've never been with a virgin before, not even when I was one. Assuming Cassie decides she's ready for the next step, do I have what it takes to make sure she doesn't regret her choice? That I don't regret it too? If Cassie and I are together, I don't want just a fling until she heads back to California. Even two days ago, that might have been okay, but it isn't now. She's under my skin and it isn't going to be easy to watch her walk away.

The responsible choice would be to part ways as friends before we make a mistake we can't take back.

Instead, I grumble, "I like Cassie. A lot. So be on your best manners, okay? She's already upset enough about all the Sunshine drama."

Blake nods, his smile fading. "Of course. We won't embarrass you, bro. At least I won't. You know Jace has a hard time not saying stupid shit."

"Is that right, smartass?" Jace launches into motion and Blake bolts for the truck with a laugh, proving some things never change.

But some things do.

If I take Cassie to bed, things between us are never going to be the same.

But so what? Some risks are worth taking and Cassie is worth this roll of the dice and so much more.

FIFTEEN

Cassie

MUCH LIKE THE FARMERS' market the other night, Sunshine Square is once again full of people. Ryan was right — half the town turned out to help with clean-up.

The other half turned out to take pictures and protest Sunshine Toys.

I park Savannah's bike against an old oak at the edge of the square and head toward Ruthie May, who's already handing out job assignments and garbage bags. I do a double-take as I realize she's standing under a birch strung with dildos tied to anal beads. It's a Sexmas tree in June.

"Such a waste, throwing away all these perfectly good products," she says. "But nobody wants to shop at a second-hand sex shop, no matter how much we clean and sanitize everything."

"Where did they all come from?" I already checked

the factory, and the building's still locked tight. We'll have to run inventory in the morning, but at first glance, it didn't look like anything was disturbed or missing.

Ruthie May hands me a garbage bag. "Been getting reports that a few people's orders never showed up. I'm wondering if one of our daily shipments got hijacked. But who'd steal a butt-load of sex toys just to dump them in a park? They could've gone to a sex therapist helping women in low-income areas. Instead, they're trash now. All trash. What is this world coming to?"

"Cassie Sunderwell. There you are."

The sheriff approaches from my left. He hitches his pants and gnaws on the corner of his mustache, and dread forces my heart low in my chest. I open my mouth to say something soothing, friendly, and Savannah-like—I swear, she could charm an alligator with a bee up its butt—but before I can speak, something beans the sheriff in the head.

Something long, tubular, rubbery, and very much resembling a penis.

"Hey, sorry," a brunette teen with a friendly smile calls. She darts past, grabs the dildo, turns, and flings it back to her friends near the slide, who all shriek and dive for the missile, tackling each other to the grass.

"What…" I start.

"They're playing dildo-ball," Ruthie May explains. "It's like football, but with—"

"This is an obscene display, Miss Sunderwell," the sheriff interrupts, rubbing the side of his face.

"I have nothing to do with that game, honest." Though I wish I had half their comfort level with handling dildos.

"I was talking about the vulgar products littering our

town," he snaps. "Things like this should never see the light of day."

"Well, that's going a little far, isn't it? There's nothing shameful about these toys. What's a shame is that we treat something natural and beautiful like it's a dirty secret," I reply, completely channeling my sister now. But it feels good. *Right*.

"There are laws and rules against dumping pornographic materials. You can't just—"

"Whoa, hold up. Are you saying you think *I* did this?" All those righteous feelings dissolve into a ball of unease.

He stares me down with that wrinkly-eyed, grandfatherly glare. "We got six news trucks from Atlanta pulling into town. Awful darn good for business to get all this free publicity, isn't it?"

"To show our town split and divided?" I point to the line of citizens marching with *Stop Corrupting Our Children* and *Sunshine Must Go* signs. "We would *never* pull a publicity stunt that would hurt anyone, including the town itself."

"Sheriff, we all know about your inferiority complex," Ruthie May interrupts, "but if you don't want those news vans getting pictures of our square dressed up for Playtime at the Kinky Corral, grab a bag and get to work."

"Where were you last night?" the sheriff asks me.

"At h-home," I stammer. "Savannah's house. All night."

"Alone?"

"She wasn't alone. She was with Ryan O'Dell." Ruthie May winks at me. "I want details on that later, by the way."

"All night?" the sheriff asks.

"*Incoming*!" someone yells.

We all duck, and another dildo whizzes over our heads.

"Ava Leigh, you play dildo-ball on your own time," Ruthie May hollers. "Right now, we need to get this square cleaned up."

"Sorry, ma'am," the teenager replies. "Can we keep a couple of these?"

"Only if you promise not to use them for anything other than dildo-ball. They're not sanitary. You understand me?"

"Yes, ma'am."

"Those are evidence," the sheriff growls.

"You've got pictures, sheriff," Ruthie May snaps. "And by now, those girls' fingerprints are all over those. Help or get out of the way."

"We'll help," a soothing, familiar voice says. Tingles race down my spine, and despite everything wrong in the square this morning, when I turn to look at Ryan, I'm smiling.

He smiles back, and my insides flip upside down. "We'll take two bags each, Ruthie May."

"Two? I'll do three before you've filled one." Blake grins at me. It takes me a minute to recognize him with the long hair, but he has the O'Dell build and smile. "Hey, Cassie. Great to see you again. Hear you're keeping this old guy in line."

"Mostly just his raccoon," I reply.

Ryan and Blake both laugh. Jace cracks a half-smile that doesn't reach his eyes.

Ruthie May smiles broadly, and I have no doubt the whole town will soon be debating how many children Ryan and I will have by the time I'm thirty.

"Miss Sunderwell," the sheriff starts again.

I shake open my trash bag. "Excuse me, sheriff. I have community service to do."

Ryan, Blake, and Jace follow me toward the end of the square near Maud and Gerald's donut shop and bakery along Main Street. They each have a trash bag in hand and another in a back pocket. The volunteers have made a lot of progress, but there's still so much to do, and no one's tackled this corner yet.

And as promised, Ryan's brought gloves.

I've never wanted to kiss a man over rubber gloves before, but I definitely want to kiss him now.

"What's with the sheriff?" he asks.

Gloves on, I bend to grab a dildo by the base with two fingers and drop it in my trash bag. "Not enough fiber in his diet?"

Blake laughs. Jace cracks another half-grin.

"If he's giving you trouble—" Ryan starts.

I grab a packet of lube, and my cheeks are on fire, but I reach for a butt plug too. "He's just doing his job."

"He should be asking to see Maud's webcam footage," Jace says, pointing to the bakery with a dildo he's just grabbed.

He looks down at what he's pointing with, sighs, and stuffs it in his trash bag.

Ryan glances back at the sheriff, then hands his bag over to Blake. "You wanted to fill three of these. Here you go."

"Ah, taking the lazy way out," Blake says with a grin.

"Helping build your character," Ryan replies.

A familiar laugh rings from across the park. Olivia's under the shelter in the center of the square, playing tug-of-war with George and a string of anal beads.

"Your raccoon's quite the ladies' man," Blake says. "Maybe you can take him on your next date."

Ryan and I share a glance. He grimaces, and I giggle. George was *not* a ladies' man last night.

"C'mon, Cassie. Let's go see Maud." He takes my garbage bag and holds it out to Jace, who's staring at Olivia with his jaw ticking. Blake notices and grabs my bag too.

"Lazy, both of you," he teases. He elbows Jace. "Earth to loverboy."

Jace jerks away. "I'm going to get a ladder," he mutters.

"I get it. Abandon the youngest. That's always how it is." If Blake's really put out, his amused grin doesn't show it.

"You're not the youngest," Ryan reminds him.

"I'm the youngest in the country at the moment. Go on, go talk to Maud while I do all the hard work."

He winks at me, and the playful banter between the two brothers makes me want to hug Savannah so badly I can hardly breathe.

I miss my sister.

"You okay?" Ryan slips an arm around my shoulders, and the pain in my lungs eases.

I nod. "Let's go see Maud. I'm not letting Savannah come home to a mess."

He hooks his hand through mine as we step over butt plugs and feather ticklers and head to the street, and an electric current shoots up my arm.

He still likes me, despite the toilet trouble.

I squeeze his hand. "Thank you."

"For rescuing you from the dildos?" he replies with a teasing grin.

"Ugh, that too."

"They really bother you."

I step over an extra-large model that looks like it

could cause some damage. "I've just never been as comfortable with talking about sex as Savannah is. I'm missing that gene, I guess. Or maybe I was old enough to understand what my parents really meant when they told us to stay away from certain people while we were on set for her show. Or maybe it's just that everything was so public when I was little, that I like privacy in everything now."

"Ah, privacy. That anonymity you love in San Francisco."

I sway into him while we step off the curb to cross the street, and the brush of our arms makes me tingle more. "Yeah. But being anonymous in a big city hasn't brought me out of my shell. I should be grateful to whoever tossed these dildos. Maybe I'll touch enough of them today to get over blushing every time I look at one."

He grins down at me. "I like your blush. In fact, I'd like to watch your whole body blush."

I bite my lip. "I'd like to enjoy my body and not worry if it's blushing or not."

"God, Cassie, now *I'm* getting a little uncomfortable."

"What? I'm sorry—*oh*."

He makes a subtle adjustment to his pants. "Don't be sorry. I like the thought of you enjoying yourself. I just like the thought of you enjoying yourself with me even more."

"Me too," I say, blushing again, though by this point I don't care.

He likes me. He really likes me and is attracted to me and maybe it's time to trust that I can handle a sexual relationship with another adult.

Maybe it's time to trust that I'm not a natural screw-up. That I *am* beautiful and special and worthy, and that I deserve happiness and pleasure.

We walk into the bakery, and my mouth waters at the scent of donuts and cinnamon rolls. Gerald looks up from behind the glass counter and gives me a squirrely eyeball. "Look who the raccoon dragged in," he grumbles.

"Morning, Gerald," Ryan says easily. "Y'all still have cinnamon rolls?"

"And donuts?" I add hopefully.

"All out," he says.

"Gerald! We are not." Maud hustles out of the kitchen, glances at my and Ryan's joined hands, and her face crinkles in a huge smile. "Coffee and treats on the house, just to apologize for *someone* being rude. Sit, sit, you two. How was your bike ride yesterday? Cassie, did you really flip upside down on the zipline? It happens, honey. And I'm sure Ryan was there to catch you."

She's piling a plate with cinnamon rolls and muffins and donuts while she talks, and we both know the price of breakfast is some good, juicy gossip. "We have to get back to the park," I tell Maud, "but we were wondering if we could see your webcam footage from last night?"

"Of course you can." She plops a second plate on the counter and turns to grab two coffee mugs. "Gerald, go get the computer."

"Ain't got anything on it," he grumbles.

"We don't know until we check, now, do we?"

SIXTEEN

Ryan

FORTY MINUTES LATER, we're back in the park with no more information than we started with, because Maud and Gerald's webcam didn't record anything last night but the scrap of black fabric someone tossed over the lens. Whoever did this knew the town well enough to know where the security cameras are.

I figured it was a local, but the confirmation of the fact still leaves a bad taste in my mouth. I've come to expect better from the citizens of Happy Cat. We gossip and take sides, but most of us have respect for the town and personal property.

News crews are set up all over the park, interviewing protesters and volunteers alike while the teens huddle behind the playground. Jace is pulling sex toy ornaments off the trees, and Blake is the proud owner of three full trash bags.

"You want to take these home?" he asks me. "Make art out of them?"

"Art?" Cassie says.

"You can't weld silicone," I tell my brother.

"Lots of handcuffs in here," he replies with a grin.

"Savannah doesn't sell handcuffs," Cassie says. "Long story involving an anti-nuke protest when she was twelve."

"So these aren't all Sunshine Toys?" Interesting.

"Some of the dildos definitely aren't, and I think the butt plugs are cheap knock-offs," Olivia announces. She points to Blake's bags. "May I please have those? I'm sorting the evidence."

"Uh, yeah." Blake's brows are up toward his hairline, which is understandable. I don't know if any of us saw Detective Olivia coming, but he recovers quickly. "Where do you want them?"

She smiles. "Over in the picnic shelter, please."

"You got it."

He hustles across the park, stopping along the way to grab more litter.

"Olivia, that's a great idea," Cassie says. "Thank you."

"Ruthie May suggested it." Olivia touches my arm. "And, Ryan, I've been meaning to talk to you. When is George Cooney's birthday?"

"Ah…sometime in April?"

"Oh, no. I was afraid of that."

Cassie presses her lips together and grabs a bag, abandoning me to pick up lube packets and errant cock rings, which is oddly arousing.

But then just about everything about Cassie is arousing.

I blink back at Olivia. "April is a bad month for raccoons?"

"I was reading his star chart. Now's a critical time for George to find a mate. If you haven't found a mating in captivity group yet, you need to, like yesterday."

"Oh. Ah, I see. Thank you."

She nods. "You're welcome."

She floats off to gather more bags of trash, and I catch up to Cassie. Her pigtails are touching the ground as she bends over to snag a trio of feather ticklers while a parade of protesters march by twenty feet away.

No More Sunshine! No More Sunshine!

"That would be really funny if it wasn't my sister they were talking about," Cassie tells me. "Here. You can put your dildo in my bag."

I drop the litter in, and we both reach for a string of anal beads on the ground.

She snorts a soft laugh. "It's like *Lady and the Tramp*, the X-rated version."

"By all means, they're yours."

We're both laughing when the sheriff ambles back over, sluggish but determined. "Miss Sunderwell, we didn't finish our conversation."

He's holding handcuffs.

Seven pairs, to be exact. Four fuzzy pink, two fuzzy black, and one fuzzy leopard print.

"Hold on just a minute," I growl.

The sheriff shoves all seven pairs into a trash bag and ignores me. "Miss Sunderwell, I need you to come with me."

"Why?" I demand.

"I didn't do this," she tells the sheriff.

"Then you won't have any issue coming on down to the station to answer a few questions."

I step between them. "You can ask her questions right here."

"It's fine, Ryan." She puts a hand on my arm, and my skin crackles with suppressed energy. I want to toss her over my shoulder, carry her to my truck, and take her away from all of this. "It's easier to talk away from all the gossip anyway."

"I'll come with you."

"No, you stay and finish cleaning up," she says. "It's okay. I'll be fine. And if I can help figure out who did this, all the better."

"Cassie—"

She goes up on tiptoe and kisses my cheek. "He's not a dildo. I can handle him."

And now I'm lightheaded.

She pulls away, fluttering her fingers. "Thank you. For everything."

Blake steps up next to me, grinning, while Cassie turns and walks away with the sheriff.

"Somebody's got it bad," he says.

Yeah. I do.

But she's not in Happy Cat to stay, and with a baby on the way, Jace is going to need me here at home more than ever. There's no future in Cassie and me.

But that won't stop me. I know that the way I know the summer sun is hot and that George won't make it out of downtown without adding another strand of anal beads to his collection.

I'M BACK on another twenty-four-hour shift Monday at the firehouse. I haven't seen Cassie since she left me in the park yesterday morning, and I'm trying to ignore the itching in my skin from wanting to confirm with my own two eyes that she's doing okay.

"Heard you and Cassie are a thing," Jojo says while we're washing the fire truck in the early morning. "And she's still planning on going back to San Francisco."

I make a noncommittal noise, because this is the part of small-town living I hate the most. I don't know what Cassie and I are—friends, yes. Attracted, yes. Beyond that? I have no idea.

But everyone's already deciding for us, and already finding the fly in our relationship ointment.

"She really get grilled by the sheriff for eight hours yesterday?"

"No." I'm not the biggest fan of Sheriff Briggs but I'm not going to lie about him. She texted me three hours after she left the park to let me know she had to do inventory at Sunshine Toys to make sure nothing involved in yesterday's defacing of downtown had come directly from the warehouse.

She refused my offer of help, so instead, I spent the afternoon coaxing George home and welding art.

Without dildos or handcuffs. I work in large reclaimed scrap from the junkyard and not much else.

Jojo's staring at me. "You two break up already?"

"What? No. We're not—she's my neighbor. We hang out. Touch her and die."

He grins. "Noted." He swipes the red truck with a rag, pausing to rub at a spot. "Did your *neighbor* spend the night in the slammer? I would've volunteered for jail if I knew I was going home to those protestors."

I grunt. "You ever wonder why so many people are opposed to the factory?"

"Sex is sacred," he says with a shrug.

"Is it? Because who's sleeping with who is a big topic around here."

Jojo frowns thoughtfully. "Would it be in bad taste to ask if you need to get laid?"

I toss a wet sponge at him. He ducks it, snickering. We both straighten when Jessie steps out of the firehouse and onto the concrete pad with us.

"You missed a spot," she says dryly.

Jojo tackles the smudge while she circles the engine. When she reaches me again, she's frowning. "Heard you're seeing Cassie Sunderwell."

"Gotta take a bio break, Chief," Jojo calls.

Chickenshit.

"We're friends," I tell the chief.

"She talk to you about the factory?"

That itch I get when one of my brothers is in trouble takes root in my spine. "Mostly about how holding down the fort here is different than programming computer games in San Francisco."

"Report came back on that lube fire."

"And?"

"Doesn't look good. There was some sabotage on bottle labels that looked pretty intentional." She leans in and touches the *C* in *Happy Cat* on the side of the truck. "Heard Savannah wants to sell the factory."

"She's gone through some big life changes," I hedge. "Cassie says she'll be back."

Jessie studies me with sharp blue eyes. She's never been one to tolerate bullshit, and I can tell she thinks I'm bullshitting her now.

"What're you getting at, Chief?" I ask.

"Factory's losing money. Worth more if it burns down than if she sells."

My fingers curl into fists, and water drips from the sponge in my hand. "Cassie and Savannah wouldn't burn down their own factory."

"Not gonna argue that. They're the last people I'd suspect." She rocks back on her heels. "Under normal circumstances, that is. But nothing about the last few months has been normal for Savannah Sunderwell. I'm reminded of that every time I pass my neighbor's sheep pen."

I shake my head. "She wouldn't burn down her own factory. Neither would Cassie."

"There anything you wouldn't do for your brothers, O'Dell?"

I think about Jace, about impending fatherhood, about him being saddled with Ginger for the rest of his life.

About what I wouldn't do for Blake. Or Clint.

It's a fuzzy, fuzzy line. But there *is* a line. "One or two things," I grit out.

"I like the Sunderwell girls. And I agree. I don't think they'd do it. But who else would?"

"There are people protesting that factory every day of the week, and even more mad at Savannah for accusing Steve of fornicating with a sheep. Better question might be *who wouldn't?*"

"Sheriff's on it," she tells me. "But if you hear anything, you let me know."

Our radios squawk to life. "Possible HAZMAT situation at Gordon's Taxidermy Shop. Station Two, respond."

We all leap for our turnout gear.

"Ten bucks says it's a live squirrel high on weed, because what other HAZMAT is he gonna have?" Jojo says as we load up. He grins. "And another ten that you and Cassie are outed as official by this time tomorrow."

"Save the gossip for the locker rooms," Jessie orders. She flips on the lights and sirens, Hank cranks the engine, and we're off.

Just a routine call on a routine day.

But after hearing that the fire at Sunshine was suspicious, and possibly arson, nothing feels routine.

This is going to be the longest shift of my life.

SEVENTEEN

Cassie

EVERYTHING IS CRAZY.

I can't believe this is my life.

Down is up and up is down and somehow I've gone from being girl voted most likely to spend a Friday night binge-playing Doctor Mario by myself to an arson suspect with the fate of a faltering sex toy company resting on my shoulders, more life drama than Kim Kardashian post sex tape, and a sort-of-maybe boyfriend who texts me on his breaks at work to let me know he's thinking of me and that I should keep my "adorable chin up."

My *adorable* chin.

Ryan thinks my chin is adorable.

"Bigger things to worry about," I grumble at my reflection in Savannah's private office bathroom. But no matter how serious I try to keep my reflection, I can't keep the smile from my lips.

And then another text pops up on my phone and my grin goes into super stretchy mode.

Ryan: Any plans for tomorrow? Jace is bringing back karaoke night at the Wild Hog. I thought you might like to go, drink a few beers, forget about sex toys for a while?

Cassie: Sounds amazing. I'll need a break from crisis mode by then. The news trucks are still outside and half my staff didn't come into work today.

Ryan: Why?

Cassie: I don't know. Ruthie May thinks maybe they're afraid of getting caught walking into a sex toy factory on TV. Most of their families know what they do for a living, but I guess some of them are keeping the Sunshine portion of their lives a secret from their friends and neighbors. I'm helping Neil out in the lab today to pick up the slack. We'll see how much I remember from high school chemistry. Hopefully I won't blow myself up along with the self-lubricating butt plug prototypes.

Ryan: Be careful. No blowing yourself up allowed. At least not until I get to hear you sing "I Touch Myself" at karaoke.

Cassie: LOL. On a cold day in hell, O'Dell. I have a go-to list of karaoke songs and that one is NOT on it.

Ryan: Can't wait to hear your go-to list. Gotta run. Break's over. Hang in there.

Cassie: Will do.

I slip my phone back into the pocket of my borrowed lab coat and practically float out of the bathroom and down the hall toward the lab, not even the smell of the pineapple lube prototype Olivia's mixing in a room the employees affectionately call "The Sex Kitchen" able to dampen my mood. Pineapple makes my tongue break out in hives and usually the scent alone is enough to make my lips itch.

But not today. Today I am bulletproof.

I know it's just a stupid crush, but it's a *mutual* crush. Ryan is into me and I'm into him and I've all but decided to go for it—to screw my courage to the sticking point and pounce on Ryan like he's a two-pound bar of chocolate at the end of a thirty-day sugar detox.

Maybe tomorrow night.

Which means I'm potentially within a day of losing my V card, a state of affairs so exciting and panic-inducing I don't notice Ruthie May waiting for me by the entrance to the lab until she seemingly materializes out of the shadows to scare me half to death.

"Oh my God!" I press a hand to my chest, where my heart is doing its best impression of a Donkey Kong hammer. "You scared me. Sorry. I was distracted."

"Understandable," Ruthie May says, her expression uncharacteristically serious. "You've got a lot on your plate these days, and I'm afraid nothin' I've got to say is going to help you any."

Stifling a groan, I ask, "Is this about the sales projections I asked for?"

Ruthie nods, her lips pruning into an unhappy pink starburst at the bottom of her lightly wrinkled face.

"Lay it on me," I say, pinwheeling one hand. "Don't sugarcoat it. I have to know how deep the doo-doo is before I can figure a way out of it."

"Well, it could be worse," Ruthie May says, before proceeding to give me the bad news. "Sales are down ten percent from this time last year, a dozen vendors have declined to renew their contracts, and apparently there was a glitch in the online ordering system that kept new customers from making profiles or being able to complete the check-out process for nearly a month. We've caught it now, but the damage has been done. I'm projecting a major cash flow problem if we can't turn things around and get more green flowing in. And I mean yesterday."

I shake my head. "But how did this happen? I thought Savannah said there was still so much room for expansion in the organic sensual product market."

"There is, but without more effective advertising we won't be the company helping people expand their sensual horizons," Ruthie May says. "Savannah's been running late night infomercial ads, but that's not where our customers are these days."

"Of course not," I say, crossing my arms at my chest. "They're online. The internet was built on porn."

Ruthie pulls a face. "We do service some of the same customers, I suppose. I've been telling Savannah to up the online advertising budget for years, but you know how much she hates InstaChat and the search engine stuff."

I bob my head back and forth, taking the measure of that information. "Well, I hate them too. Their advertising costs are through the roof these days and the return on investment can be hard to measure. But there are other places to advertise. Even other mediums."

"Like what?" Ruthie asks, hugging her folder to her chest, curiosity sparking in her eyes.

"Like store apps for your smartphone," I say, genuine excitement flickering to life inside me as a spark of potential genius pops into my head, along with the realization that though I miss San Francisco, I haven't been daydreaming about the next edition of my company's *Vikings in…* game series. It's like I've needed something else to spark my creative juices. "Or…" I bite my lip, not wanting to jinx the idea by throwing it out into the world without figuring out how to pitch it properly.

Ruthie May laughs. "Oh, girl, I don't know what's going through your head, but I like it. It looks like a good time."

"I think it will be." I grin. "Let me do a little research and I'll get back to you. Thanks for the update." I wander into the lab, my wheels turning as I consider how best to turn buying sex toys into a game people don't ever want to stop playing.

I'm not a hundred percent sure how best to approach this, but I know one thing for sure—dildo football has to be a part of it.

If you can't beat 'em, join 'em, and sell them the best dang organic lube available on the market while you're at it.

EIGHTEEN

Ryan

BY THE TIME I finally get to the Wild Hog Tuesday night, I'm itchy and desperate to see Cassie.

I should've been here half an hour ago, but George burrowed into an open peanut butter jar he found in the trash behind Maud and Gerald's bakery, and I had to give him a bath to get the peanut butter off his fur before he tried to lick himself clean, which would've resulted in peanut butter hairballs all over my carpet.

And then I had to give myself a bath to recover from giving George a bath, because I refuse to see Cassie smelling like wet peanut butter trash panda.

It's been over forty-eight hours since I've seen her in person—not that I'm counting—and I need to know that she's okay. Need it badly.

I finally hustle into the bar a quarter after six. But even my eagerness to see Cassie, takes a backseat to abject horror when I realize what I'm seeing. And hearing.

Ruthie May is on the makeshift stage in the corner, wailing away.

To…"I Touch Myself."

She's also…touching herself. With one hand resting low on her belly, below the waistband of her linen granny pants, but not so low that the sheriff will have to intervene for public indecency.

But low enough to imply what she's headed home to do.

I want to be happy for her, but I'm leaning toward joining Emma June in hiding out in a booth with a napkin over my head until it's over. Not that the napkin is helping much with Tucker sitting next to Emma, holding up his fist, pointer and pinky extended, headbanging to the music. "You go, Ruthie May!" he hollers.

I hope Ruthie May has lots of sex.

I hope my parents do too.

I also hope to never bear witness to their sexy time private lives. Knowing it happens and seeing the gyrating on stage are two different things. Forever and ever amen.

Someone bumps into me from behind, and I realize I've stopped dead in front of the door.

"Sorry," I start, then have to school my expression so I don't curl my lip.

"O'Dell," Steve says. Savannah's ex is in a cowboy hat, a white button-down shirt, blue jeans, and—are those Italian loafers?

They are.

The dude's wearing pretentious business shoes with his bar-hopping Wranglers.

Is it any wonder he gives me bad vibes?

But I nod back, because it's polite. "Bennington."

Behind us, Ruthie May croons about what she thinks about when she does things I *don't* want to think about, and Steve's entire face wrinkles in disgust. "This town's going to hell," he mutters.

"She's just having fun, man," I say.

He snorts and his dark brown eyes skim me up and down. I've heard women swoon over those eyes and the rest of the man packaged up along with them, but Steve's gaze makes my skin crawl. "Didn't know you were one of the freaks, O'Dell. Figured you had more sense than that."

I start to crack that men with glass sheep should know better than to throw stones, but I refuse to sink to this douchebag's level.

So I shrug, forcing a tight smile. "Just believe in live and let live."

Steve's bottom lip pushes out as he nods. "I get it. I like to do good when I can too."

I do not roll my eyes.

But it's hard.

Really hard.

"I'll give you a heads-up," he says, dropping his voice as he adds, "don't get in too deep with my ex's sister, okay? The Sunderwell girls are a good time until you put a ring on that crazy. Then it's just nuts and cocoa puffs all the way down the line. Way more trouble than any pussy is worth, you feel me?"

My jaw clenches so tight something clicks near my ear as my hands curl into fists at my sides. But this snot weasel is as shitty at reading nonverbal cues as he is at keeping his marriage vows.

"Just come and go, if you get me." He winks. "Come. And go."

My fist is about to come and go—into his smarmy gut

and back out again—when someone calls his name from the bar.

"Lance! What's up, brother? Later, O'Dell." Steve brushes past me, knocking my arm with his shoulder as he bolts for more socially elite company.

"Hopefully much later, you fucking asshole," I mutter.

I'm considering texting Cassie and suggesting a change of venue—neither of us are Steve fans, after all—when a commotion at the back room catches my attention. I turn, and instantly the asshole is forgotten, and my heart feels ten years younger. I couldn't hold back my smile if I tried.

There she is.

My Cassie.

She's at the Ms. Pac-Man arcade game in back, spinning in a circle to take a round of high-fives from a motley mix of townspeople. Her cheeks are flushed, her eyes alight with joy, her hair in twin braids that are as sexy as they are innocent, and I can't wait to be close to her.

As close as I can get.

I'm across the bar, heading into the crowd around her before I realize I've moved.

"Ryan! Hey! Everything turn out okay with George?" she asks when I reach her side.

I don't answer.

Instead, I bend and capture her lips with mine, circling my arms about her waist and pulling her in for a long, lingering kiss that stirs something deep in my chest even as it sends my cock into celebration mode.

Her hands drift up to clutch at my shoulders while she kisses me back, her tongue gliding against mine, her sweet nose brushing my cheek.

Forget a night out.

I'm taking her home. To my place.

I pull away from the kiss with a soft groan.

Cassie's eyes are dark, her eyelids low. She licks her bottom lip and gives me an almost shy smile. "Hi," she whispers.

"Hi."

I'm grinning like an idiot, and I don't care. Whispers of *I knew it!* and *This is sooo going on InstaChat* and *Way to go, O'Dell!* are filtering around us, but we both ignore them.

"That's quite the congratulations for a high score in Ms. Pac-Man," Cassie says with a sultry wink that puts a new kind of hum in my veins. One that says I'm a complete and total goner for this woman. "Or was that a pre-emptive *I'm sorry* kiss because you think you can do better?"

"Is that a challenge, Cassandra Sunderwell?"

"Maybe," she says coyly. She swings her hips and grins. "And if you want to know if that's a roll of quarters in my pocket or if I'm happy to see you, the answer to both questions is yes."

I crack up, because she's funny and perfect and how did I get to be the lucky guy she's smiling at with stars in her eyes tonight? "Yeah, that's a challenge," I tell her, then I lean in so only she can hear me. "How about some stakes here? Winner gets breakfast in bed?"

"That's hardly fair, since you don't stand a chance."

"You're probably correct, but I don't mind losing, since I'd still be getting breakfast with you."

She giggles, and I reach into her pocket, where there is indeed a roll of quarters.

The music ends to a weak spatter of applause. "Thank you, Ruthie May," Blake says into the microphone. "Next up is Olivia Moonbeam, singing 'Call Me Maybe.'"

A few groans break out, but most of the crowd

around Cassie and me breaks up and heads for the main dining area. Olivia might pick ridiculously perky songs, but she's got an incredible voice.

"C'mon." Cassie tugs me to face the machine. "Let's see what you've got, O'Dell."

"Other than a desperate desire to take you back to my place?" I ask.

She blushes, but she also smiles bigger. "We'll get there. You have to woo me properly first."

I like this flirty side of her. "You're on." I drop a quarter into the machine.

"And you're off to a good start," she tells me while she loops an arm around my waist and leans her head on my arm.

A camera flashes and clicks, and I suddenly realize it isn't the first time I've heard that sound. There were a decent number of clicks snapping away while I was kissing Cassie hello.

I drop my hands from the game controllers and turn to her. "I'm sorry. The gossip—I didn't think—I just wanted to kiss you. But there are probably pictures and I'm guessing they'll be on InstaChat before we leave here tonight."

She shrugs, surprising me. "There are far worse things than having people think I'm such a sex goddess Happy Cat's hottest fireman can't resist me."

"Well, you *are* a sex goddess. But you'd better tell me the name of this fireman so I can kick his ass."

She laughs, and it's better music than anything we're getting here tonight. "Ms. Pac-Man just got eaten by a ghost. In level *one*. Thus far, you are failing to impress me with your video game skills, Mr. Hot Fireman."

I dutifully put another quarter in the machine. "I'm better at Out Run than Ms. Pac-Man," I confess.

She glances past me at the next arcade game down with its gas pedal and steering wheel. "Oh, the car racing game?"

"Yep." I fiddle the knob on the console, steering Ms. Pac-Man away from a killer ghost and completely missing a turn in a process. "I can outdrive you any day of the week, pigtails."

"Is that commentary on my handling of my bicycle?" She brushes her breast against me, I get distracted, and once again, Ms. Pac-Man is toast.

"Do I need to get behind you and show you how to handle that joystick?" she asks.

Did she just…

She did. She made a sex joke. I arch a brow in her direction. "Cassandra Sunderwell, have you been practicing your dirty talk?"

She lifts her chin, her cheeks that shade of pink that's both adorable and a little heartbreaking. I wish there was something I could do to help make her more at ease with talking about sex and sex toys and all the rest of it.

"No," she says, "but I've been doing…other things. Sexy type things…"

Forget the beers and the Ms. Pac-Man. We're getting out of here and going to my place *right now*.

Before the sheriff arrests *me* for indecency.

I turn to tell her we're leaving as Blake emerges from the back hallway. "Hey, there you two are. You get a beer yet, Ry? Gonna need it. You're up next for karaoke."

"No, we're—" I start, but Cassie claps her hands.

"Oh, good! I love karaoke. Thanks, Blake. You're officially my second-favorite O'Dell brother."

"And you're my first official favorite O'Dell brother girlfriend," he replies.

Cassie doesn't correct him.

Neither do I.

And five minutes later, we're both being shuffled to the stage. "Are you sure you want to karaoke with me? I'm not great."

"Good. That's the trick," she whispers. "You sing really badly, and then they don't ever ask you to do it again. We're doing Three Dog Night's 'Joy To The World.' Do you know that one?"

"Jeremiah was a bullfrog? Of course."

"Awesome. Follow my lead, and sing really, really bad."

I laugh and I follow her lead.

And we sing really, really badly.

So badly, we get booed off the stage.

But it comes with a round of nachos on the house to thank us for shutting up, and then Ruthie May buys us a round, followed by Blake buying us another round, and before long, we're both tipsy.

Laughing.

Telling stories about childhood.

Recreating our scenes from *Romeo and Juliet* without actually remembering any of our lines except the one that comes right before the kiss.

And for the first time in a long time, there's nowhere else in the world I'd rather be. Even as it becomes clear that I'm not taking Cassie home while we're both buzzed, I'm so damned happy I can't stop smiling.

"Incoming!" A sudden shout from the front of the bar makes us all turn to face the entrance to see two teenage girls tossing dildos at a couple of Stetson-wearing boys at a front booth.

"Five points!" one shouts, high-fiving the other, who giggles as she points to the now pink-cheeked cowboys.

"You should see your face! Three extra points our team for blushing on the sidelines."

"Won't be on the sidelines for long," the blond boy says, grabbing the dildos from his chip basket and heading out the door, chasing the girls down the street with a grin.

The remaining boy thunks a palm against his forehead in mortification and everyone around us bursts into giggles. Including Cassie, but she also puts her hands to her cheeks. Even inebriated, the unexpected dildo assault makes her blush.

And suddenly, I know exactly what I have to do about that.

A plan takes shape in my head, and it's so perfect, I can't wait to start putting it into action.

And I will.

Just as soon as I've walked my tipsy girl home and tucked her safely into bed.

NINETEEN

*From the texts of Cassie Sunderwell and
Savannah Sunderwell*

Cassie: I'm going to ask you three questions, and I need you to say yes to all of them.

Savannah: Yes.

Cassie: You have to hear them first!

Savannah: Why? If you need me to say yes, then I have to say yes, so why ask me the questions in the first place? And honestly, I'd rather not hear the questions if they have anything to do with Sunshine Toys.
I saw what happened.
The Dildo-pocalypse in the square.
It made the news all the way over here. My new boss is going to flip out if he realizes I'm the "idiot American" who thought starting a sex toy business in a small town was a good idea.

Cassie: Hold the phone and wait just a second. What are you talking about? What new boss? You're the boss!

Savannah: No, you're the boss, an arrangement we both agreed to when I decided to run away from home. But it's okay if the operation fails, Cass. I seriously don't mind. I'll just quietly go bankrupt and start over.

Cassie: No one is going bankrupt! That's what I'm texting about. I've got an idea that might save the company! Maybe even make it more profitable than ever before!

Savannah: That's great. As soon as you start making big bucks, I'll sign the entire operation over to you so you can reap the rewards of your hard work. Until such time, however, we should keep everything in my name so I don't drag you down into the gutter with me.

Cassie: No one's going to the gutter. We're going to the playground.

Savannah: You lost me… But in a weirdly appropriate way since I happen to be at a playground right now with the adorable little girl I'm nannying. Kids love slides, Cassie. Like…LOVE them a ridiculous amount.

Cassie: Well, of course they do. What's not to love about a slide? And you're a nanny? How on earth did that happen? Have you ever spent quality time with children? In your entire life?

Savannah: No, I haven't. Not even when I was a kid. I was always working or hiding out with you in my trailer

because we were the weirdos from the South who didn't fit in with the Hollywood elite.
I'm sad that we missed so much slide time.
I feel especially bad that you missed so much of it on my account. You should have been able to run wild and free, big sister, and slide to your heart's content. Do you hate me for stealing your childhood?

Cassie: You didn't steal my childhood! Lol. Don't be crazy. I had a great time on set with you. Well, most of the time, except that summer I farted in front of the stunt double I liked after eating too many burritos from the food truck.
And I never would have learned to code if I hadn't been in L.A. They didn't have summer coding classes in Happy Cat back then.

Savannah: They still don't, do they?

Cassie: Hmmm… Maybe not. That's something I should check into. These kids need a leg up on getting with the times. Though they are a creative group. The rules this group of teen girls just texted me for Dildo Football are hysterical. I'll have to call it something different in the app, though. Give it a snappier name, add in some extra levels, maybe a dildo doing a touchdown dance when you score.

Savannah: What are you talking about? Do you have a fever? What's all this talk of frolicking with dildos? Not that I don't approve, you know I do, but you're giving me whiplash.

Cassie: I know, I'm still a little uncomfortable with it all,

but it's how I'm going to save the company! I'm going to gamify your advertising by making a Sunshine Toys app packed with mini games, special coupons, and in-app purchases. We'll make it fun and sparkly, just like you, and appeal directly to your younger consumers. Looking at Ruthie May's data, you're missing nineteen to twenty-five-year-olds, which is HUGE.
And I realized, after I thought about it, that if I didn't know you personally, I would have no idea that Sunshine Toys exists. Which is sad, because I would want to know. I would want to know that there's this amazing, sex-positive, body-positive, woman- and nature-positive company out there that wants to help me discover all the ways my body can experience pleasure.

Savannah: Oh my God. You did it, didn't you? You had sex. With Ryan O'Dell!

Cassie: No, I haven't. But that reminds me! Three questions! One — do I have your permission to create a Sunshine Toys app and spend approximately twenty-five percent of your marketing budget to get the word out about our fun new toy?

Savannah: Knock yourself out. It's not like things can get much worse.

Cassie: Yay! Two — are you comfortable with me staying at your place a few extra weeks? I already worked out a remote working arrangement with my boss and I shouldn't have a problem juggling both jobs. I'm not due to work lead on a game for another six months.

Savannah: Of course. Stay as long as you like. Now get to

the good stuff. I'm assuming number three is the juicy one?

Cassie: Yes. It is. Can I pretty please have your blessing to bang your neighbor? I know that might make things awkward for you when you get home, but he's so wonderful, Van. So sexy and sweet and funny and kind and I truly cannot imagine a better De-Virginizer showing up in my life. I don't want to let this chance pass me by.

Savannah: The De-Virginizer. Ew. It sounds like the Terminator—I'll be back! In your vagina!

Cassie: Can you be serious, please? This is a big deal for me. I'm ready, dude. It finally feels right, you know?

Savannah: Then you should go for it, doll face. Rush headlong into love and squeeze every bit of joy you can out of it before it goes rotten.

Cassie: No one said anything about love. This is sex. Momentous, first-time sex, yes. But still, purely physical.

Savannah: Right. Because when I'm looking for a fuck buddy, I always go on and on about how sweet and funny he is. *eye roll emoji* You're falling for him, Cassie. And that's okay. Just go in with your eyes open and make sure he's on the same page before you take a leap off the love high-dive. Make sure there's water in the pool, you know?

Cassie: I think there is, Van. I think there's water. He likes me too. Like, maybe even REALLY likes me.

Savannah: And why wouldn't he? You're wonderful and I love you. Got to go, Beatrice wants to play ninja rabbits with rabies.

Cassie: Sounds fun.

Savannah: Oh, it is. Maybe the most fun I've had in years. Love you! Be safe! Use condoms! Lots and lots of condoms! With lube!

TWENTY

Ryan

"KEEP 'EM CLOSED." I shuffle forward across the grass at the back of my property behind Cassie, my fingers cupped around her eyes. "No peeking. Peeking is cheating."

She laughs. "How can I peek with your big mitts covering half my face? Has anyone ever told you that you have ridiculously giant hands?"

"All the time," I say. "Usually whenever they see me holding my massive firehose."

She giggles again, a sweet, happy sound that makes me want to keep her here with me forever, far from downtown and the sex toy factory and all the uptight assholes who are doing their best to make her visit to Happy Cat as miserable as possible. Coming home should be as fun as karaoke night was, which is why I spent the entire afternoon getting busy with my welding iron and a pile of scrap metal creating my most ambitious trash sculpture to date.

All in the name of helping Cassie get more comfortable with sex.

While I was soldering away in the shade, there was no doubt in my mind that Cassie was going to love her surprise.

But now, as we circle around the shed where I keep the smaller pieces of scrap I salvage from the junkyard and the ten-foot monstrosity comes into view, I wonder if I might have taken things too far.

Cassie has an incredible sense of humor, and the beer convinced me this was a good idea, but…

That thing is gigantic. And obnoxious. And definitely *not* going to be selected for inclusion in the annual art walk.

"Are we almost there? Seriously, I'm dying of curiosity," Cassie says, twiddling her fingers on the backs of my hands. Even that innocent touch is enough to make me ache to hold her, to kiss her, to show her that pleasure is nothing to be intimidated by.

Hopefully my surprise will help with that.

Or it will make her think I'm out of my fucking mind.

Either way, there's no turning back now.

"We're here. Your surprise." I pull my hands away, my gaze fixed on her face and my breath held as I wait for her response.

She blinks. Then blinks again, three times in rapid succession, as if she can't quite believe her eyes. Her lips part and a soft, shocked sound escapes from deep in her chest. She blinks again. Then again.

Finally, her lips tremble into a light-up-the-world smile and I release the breath I'm holding.

She gets it. She totally gets it, which makes me ridiculously happy.

Cassie's gaze shifts my way, her expression vulnerable in a way I haven't seen many times before. "You made me a giant metal dildo."

I nod seriously. "I did."

"With googly eyes and...." She glances back at my creation, brows furrowed. "And horns? Are those horns?"

"I was thinking antennae, but horns work too."

"It's...beautiful," she says, her eyes shining. "It's the most beautiful thing anyone has ever made for me. Thank you."

I lift a hand, cupping her cheek. "It's hideous. *You're* beautiful. And you've got no reason to be intimidated by a bunch of stupid sex toys." I nod toward the pile of scrap next to my creation. "That's why you're going to make one too."

"One what?"

"A giant metal dildo," I say. "I'll help with the welding, but you can put the pieces together any way you like."

She arches a brow, her pretty mouth curving on one side. "Really?"

"Really."

"Can I give it a face, too? A clown face with a big red nose?"

"Sure. I've got red paint. But that sounds like it might skew scary, doesn't it?"

Cassie steps closer, mischief creeping into her expression. "Why, Mr. O'Dell, are you afraid of clowns?"

"*Afraid* isn't the word I would use," I say, slipping an arm around her waist.

"Then what word would you use?"

"I'm respectful of their space. They don't get too close

to me, I don't get too close to them, and no one ends up locked in an abandoned lion cage at the back of the carnival while a serial killer in floppy shoes sharpens his collection of polka dot-handled hunting knives."

She laughs, that rich, carefree laugh that is quickly becoming one of my favorite sounds in the world. "That's a very detailed fantasy."

"Nightmare," I correct. "Recurring. I read too much Stephen King as a kid. But don't tell anyone. I'm trying to maintain my rep as an adult who can be trusted to rush bravely into burning buildings."

Cassie's gaze softens. "I won't tell anyone. And I think you're very brave." She lifts a hand, running her fingers gently over the scar on my cheek. "Jojo stopped by for a lube refill for his girlfriend today. He told me about the fire at the welding shop. How you went in to save your friend and they almost weren't in time to get you out."

I shrug uncomfortably. "Jojo talks too much."

She frowns. "I'm sorry. If you don't want to talk about it, that's fine. I didn't mean to pry."

"No, it's not that, it's just..." I hug her closer. "It was a long time ago. And it was scary, yeah, but it also changed my life for the better. That night is what inspired me to become a firefighter. And fighting fires is my soul work, you know? Something I know makes a difference in people's lives every single day."

She nods. "Yeah. It does. You're a hero."

I scoff, rolling my eyes. "I don't know about that."

"I do," she says, without a trace of doubt. "You're my hero anyway. I touched twenty-seven dildos today and only blushed fire engine red once. Never could have happened without you."

I smile. "And now we're going to finish the job of getting you dildo comfy. Ready to get your art on?" I'd much rather carry her inside and kiss every sexy inch of her, but crazy as this is, I think it's going to help her.

Cassie nods, propping her hands on her hips as she surveys the pile of scrap. "Ready. Where do I start?"

"I'll get you gloves to protect your hands and then you can sort through the pieces. I like to lay my sculptures out on the grass first, in a kind of flattened 3D style, then assemble from the base up, tweaking as I go. But not everyone's brain works that way. Blake likes to make heads first, then bodies, and attach the arms and legs last." I jab a thumb toward the fence at the back of my two acres. "Those are his. The metal scarecrows. The rest of the redneck sculpture garden is my stuff."

I wave in the general area beneath the ancient apple trees, where my initial Wizard of Oz tribute from a few years back—Dorothy and her friends populate the center of the space—eventually turned into a full-fledged fictional characters-made-of-scrap party. I've got all our favorites from when my brothers and I were growing up as well as a special request from the kids down the street, who insisted no sculpture garden would be complete without a Pikachu.

"Wow. You're both so talented." Cassie bites her lip. "Just to warn you, I'm consistently awful at artistic things. I'd hate to ugly things up around here."

"It's okay," I assure her. "Art is about the fun, not the end result. And I'll have to hide both of these in the shed after we're done, anyway. The kids from the neighborhood like to hang out here, and I'm not ready to explain dildos to them. Or to their parents."

Cassie points a finger at my chest. "Good call. That would be an excellent way to get even more people waving pitchforks and trying to run Sunshine out of town."

"Which we're not going to think about tonight," I gently remind her. "Tonight is for happy things."

Her eyes meet mine, a look in those rich chocolate depths I can't decipher.

"What?" I finally ask. "Do I have paint on my nose?"

She shakes her head. "No. You have handsome on your nose. And I was just thinking that…" She shrugs. "Well, I was thinking that I'm pretty much always happy when I'm with you."

That does it. I can't resist going in for a kiss.

I thread my fingers through her silky hair and slant my lips over hers, kissing her with the late afternoon sun warming our faces. But it isn't the summer heat that makes my blood run hot. It's this woman, who I'm finding it harder and harder to imagine letting go of.

At least not anytime soon.

"I have an idea," she whispers against my lips.

"What's that?" I ask.

"I'm not going to give it a clown face. I'm going to do something even better. But it's going to be a surprise."

I smile down at her. "Then let's glove up and get going."

Thirty minutes later, Cassie has all the pieces for the base of her own giant metal dildo laid out on the grass. She hands them to me one at a time, giving instructions on how she wants them joined together, but insisting she isn't ready to learn to weld just yet.

"Baby steps," she says, handing me a faded blue piece of sheet metal she's just finished hammering into a half circle on one of my shapers. "I'll learn to play with fire next time."

Next time. I like the sound of that. I like it so much that I have to kiss her again. When we come up for air this time, her lips are swollen and there's a hungry look in her eyes that makes me want to offer myself up as her appetizer, main course, and dessert.

"I just realized something," she says. "I won't be able to surprise you with the face unless I weld it myself."

I arch a brow. "That's what you were thinking about while I was kissing you?"

Lids drooping to half-mast, she shakes her head. "No. That wasn't what I was thinking about. That part came after. During the kissing part I was thinking of…other things."

"What kind of other things?"

"Help me figure out how to make my surprise," she says, lifting her nose into the air. "And maybe I'll tell you."

I smile. "I've got super glue. Won't hold it forever, maybe, but it'll do until I can solder it all in place later."

Cassie claps her hands. "Perfect!"

And it is perfect.

Every minute with her.

By the time the sun slips behind the horizon, we're nearly finished. I get to work on clean up, collecting the leftover scrap and disposing of the pieces too small to recycle into something new, while Cassie puts on her finishing touches.

"Okay, you can look now," she says, granting me permission to check out her masterpiece. The moment I lay eyes on the thing I burst into laughter. I can't help it, but thankfully Cassie seems pleased by my response.

"It's a unicorn," she announces happily. "A unicorn dildo!"

"I see that," I say, still chuckling. "I like the rainbow mane."

"The paint is a little sloppy since I was in a hurry," she says, grinning up at the multi-colored spikes she's affixed to the head. "But I kind of like it. The messiness is working for me."

"Me too, but you didn't have to rush. I've got lamps in the shed. We could have turned them on and kept working after dark."

Cassie turns to me, threading her fingers together in front of her paint-spattered cut-off jeans, holding my gaze a long moment before she says in a softer voice, "I didn't want to keep working after dark."

My pulse leaps in my throat. "No?"

She shakes her head as she starts across the grass toward me, every step making my heart beat faster. "No. I wanted to do…other things after dark."

"Toast marshmallows over my fire pit?"

She shakes her head, stepping deliberately over a hammer I missed during clean up. "Two guesses left."

"Help take George for his evening walk?" I ask, my voice going husky as she stops in front of me, close enough for me to count the specks of blue paint scattered across the bridge of her nose and dotted on her glasses. She's so cute, it's almost painful to look at her, and I have to fight the urge to imagine her wearing those paint specks and nothing else.

I'm pretty sure I'm reading the look on her face correctly, but I don't want to make any assumptions or do anything to pressure her into making a decision she's not ready to make yet. I want this to be her call.

"One guess left," she coos, clucking her tongue. "Really, Ryan, you're pretty awful at guessing games."

"I am." I tuck a lock of hair behind her ear, letting my fingers linger on the delicate skin behind it before I pull away. "Maybe if I had a hint?"

A hint…" Her lashes sweep down, fanning across her flushed cheeks before she looks back up at me, a Mona

Lisa smile on her face. "What has two arms, two legs, and would like to wrap all of them around you as soon as possible? Hint—her name isn't George."

"Could it be Cassandra Mae Sunderwell?"

She nods, her face going pinker but her gaze never wavering from mine. "It is. Take me inside? I'm ready to learn what all the fuss is about."

"You're sure?" I ask, fighting to keep my hands to myself until every shred of doubt is swept away.

"I'm sure," she says, sliding her hands around my neck.

A beat later, my lips are on hers as I sweep her into my arms.

TWENTY-ONE

Cassie

I'M breathless and drunk on Ryan's kisses even before we make it to his bedroom. He kicks the door shut and settles me on top of a homemade quilt on his king-size bed, following me down and aligning his body with mine.

"I can't get enough of you," he murmurs as he strokes my hair back and recaptures my mouth with his.

Everything about him engulfs me. His woodsy scent mixed with heat and metal. His touch—both the gentleness of his fingers along my neck and the scratch of his stubble against the sensitive skin around my mouth. His taste, rich and intoxicating.

The solid strength of his body.

The soft moan of pleasure as I touch my tongue to his.

Anticipation bubbles through my veins and channels between my legs. I'm not nervous—just excited.

This feels so *right*. Finally right. Finally everything I've wanted and more.

Like maybe the reason I'm still a virgin is that I was waiting for this. For today.

For *him*.

He pulls out of the kiss and gazes down at me. "If this is too much—if you want me to stop—any time—"

"Please don't stop." I run my hands down his neck, over his wide shoulders, and pluck at his tee shirt. "And please get rid of this. I want to see you."

He reaches behind his head, pulling his tee off in one smooth motion. "Anything else?" he asks with a grin, as I breathlessly take in the sight of his bare skin. He has a light dusting of dark hair across his broad chest and a firefighter badge tattooed over his heart. I trace the ridges of his ribs down to the sculpted beauty of his hard stomach while he leans beside me, letting me inspect him.

"Wow," I whisper.

"Careful." He pulls my knuckles to his lips and presses the sweetest kiss to them. "That kind of praise could give a man a big head."

My gaze drifts lower with a grin. "Really?"

He laughs and tugs at the hem of my shirt. "Oh, yeah. And you're overdressed."

"Can you help me? I think I forgot how to undress myself."

I bat my eyelashes like a big dork, but he just smiles wider, his eyes going smoky and that bulge pressing tighter against my thigh. "It would be my pleasure."

He scoots down the bed, settles between my legs, and pushes my shirt up, revealing my belly button. Inch by inch, he kisses and licks his way up my chest, pushing my shirt up as he goes, until I'm writhing under his touch.

He pulls my nipple into his mouth through my lace

bra, and sheer pleasure flutters from my breasts to my core, pulsing deep inside me, more intense than anything I've ever experienced. My legs tighten around him instinctively.

"More?" he asks, rubbing at my other nipple through my bra.

"More," I gasp. I want so much more. And I'm too high on the sensations he's sparking throughout my body to form any other words.

"Time for this to go." He pushes my shirt over my head, stroking my arms as he pulls them from the sleeves, his rough fingertips the perfect mix of gentle and possessive, arousing and soothing. He glides his body along mine, settling his thick, hard cock between my legs, and capturing my lips in a kiss that utterly owns me.

I'm wrapped in Ryan, lost and found in him, and I don't want to be anywhere else.

Ever.

Not San Francisco. Not Savannah's house.

Not even the next room over.

I just want to be here, with him, this man who feels like home.

"You," he rasps out as he breaks the kiss, "are an addictive goddess."

My fingers dance along the hot, flat planes of his chest and I arch closer to the bulge pressing between my thighs, lifting my hips to rub it against where I ache. "More," I plead.

"Trust me?" he asks while he kisses a trail down my neck.

"Yes."

He slides back down my body, and I whimper when his hips lift off mine.

But when he pops the button on my jeans and lowers

my zipper, licking and stroking my lower belly with his tongue, I'm back in heaven.

"Pink lace," he murmurs while he nibbles at the top of my panties and angles my hips to pull my pants down to my thighs. "You match."

"I was hoping for more of a reaction than—Oh God. *Ryan!*"

His name is a strangled cry as he licks me through my panties.

It's the most exquisite torture I've ever had. I want him to lick me more, but I also want *more*. Of everything.

"I've been dreaming about this forever." His breath heats the lace covering my sensitive flesh. "And reality is so much better than I've ever imagined."

He strokes me through the lace with his tongue again, and I moan. I'm gripping his hair, the coarse thickness as perfect as everything about him.

"I'm going to take your panties off and make you come in my mouth, Cassie," he says. "Sound good?"

I think I answer something like *yes*. My heart is racing, my tongue is dry, and Ryan's gliding my panties down over my hips. He pulls my shoes off, then my pants, until I'm lying naked on his bed—except for my bra—with cool air drifting over my skin, a sharp contrast to the hot wetness between my legs.

And then his mouth is back where I need it so desperately, licking and kissing before he pauses at the top to suckle my clit into his mouth.

Everything's so new, but so *right*.

The burst of pleasure making me ache in my core, need coiling deep inside me while he suckles and strokes me and makes love to me with his mouth until I'm gasping for breath and arching off the bed, my release building thick and heavy under his talented tongue.

"More—yes—*there*," I moan.

And suddenly I'm shattering.

Muscles I didn't know I have tighten and release, my inner walls clenching, and bliss rockets through my veins. My thighs clamp around Ryan's head as I ride out the new sensations overtaking my body.

So *this* is what the fuss is about.

The natural high of ultimate pleasure shared with someone else. Except it's not *enough*.

I want to share even more with him. I want him inside me.

"More?" I ask.

He chuckles and lifts his head. "That wasn't enough?"

"I haven't had *you* yet," I answer, suddenly shy. "I mean, that was—you were—amazing, but I want—I want *everything*, Ryan."

I freeze, because it strikes me a moment too late that he might think I mean in *and* out of bed, but his smile's growing, and his eyes are getting darker, his lids heavy.

"I mean, if you can do *that* with your mouth, then when you use your…"

"My…?" he prompts.

He's not laughing. He's watching me intently, and I swear he *smells* turned on.

"Your cock," I whisper. "I want to feel your cock inside me."

He swears softly, and an instant later, his pants and underwear go flying across the room. I gasp as I take in the sight of his fully naked body—the tight hips, the hollow of his belly button, the very large, very thick, *very* solid length of his cock.

He snags a condom from the bedside table, and I find my coordination to reach for it, plucking it from his fingers. "May I?"

"Of course," he says, voice husky.

I want to inspect every inch of him—and there are a lot of inches—but just the sight of his engorged head and erect length is making me ache with emptiness.

There's no fear, despite his size, because I know as surely as I know my own name that he'll fit perfectly.

And he'll be gentle.

I grip him, shocked at how smooth his skin is, and tentatively trace the tip.

Such soft skin over hot iron.

"Cassie," he grinds out. "If you don't stop—"

I smile, because I might be a virgin who balks at speaking the word *dildo* aloud, but I still hear things, and I've read my share of romance novels. "Ryan O'Dell, am I making you lose control?"

"Yes," he grunts.

His eyes flutter shut again, but not before I catch sight of them crossing.

I roll the condom down his length, and as soon as I'm done, he pounces, trapping me against the bed. "Give me just a minute," he says.

"I—" I start, but then he's sucking on that magic spot between my neck and shoulders while he unhooks my bra and sneaks a hand under one cup to roll my nipple between his thumb and finger, and I suddenly need a minute too.

"You are so damn sexy," he tells me.

His cock is pressing against my entrance, but he's not making any effort to rush. I tilt my hips, my body outside of my control, instinct taking over as he whispers praise of my breasts, my skin, my *sweet, delicious* pussy.

He sucks my bare nipple into his mouth, and my hips come off the bed at the intensity of the pleasure rocketing to my newly-awakened orgasm muscles. "*Ryan*," I cry.

"You are so beautiful," he whispers. "So perfect."

He presses a kiss to the hollow between my breasts as he pushes into me, slowly stretching my inner walls apart, one careful inch at a time. I open my legs wider and angle my hips to take him deeper, wonder and joy filling my entire being as deeply and fully as he's filling my body.

"God, Cassie, you're so perfect." The strained reverence in his voice nearly brings tears to my eyes. "So tight. Are you okay?"

"*More*," I say, because I don't think I can force anything else out around this lump in my throat.

I grasp his firm ass cheeks and pull while I open myself fully to him.

I want *all* of him.

I want to feel him in my soul.

He lifts his head and holds my gaze as he fully sheaths himself inside me. He pulls almost all the way out, then glides back in, easier this time. My breath catches as he hits a sensitive spot inside me, and he slows, stroking inside me to hit it again.

"There?" he asks.

"Oh, yes," I moan.

He catches one of my hands and lifts it over my head, threading his fingers through mine while he pumps into me, the slow, luxurious strokes giving way to frenzied thrusts that build that coil tight deep inside me again.

He's still watching me, watching my eyes, his lips parted, a sheen of perspiration forming on his forehead. "Cassie," he gasps. "Baby, I can't—I can't hold out much longer. I want—I want you to come. I want this to be good for you."

He drives into me one more time, and with his big, strong body against mine, his solid cock hitting that magic spot inside me, and the intensity in his expression while he holds me captive with his eyes, I fall over the edge.

Again.

My walls clench and spasm around him, my climax hitting so hard and tight that everything beyond our connection disappears. "*Ryan!*" I gasp.

He cries out my name and throws his head back, and I press my hips as close to his as I can get.

It's just him and me, together, riding wave after wave of pleasure, taking us deeper under this spell, and I don't ever want this to stop.

Ever.

Never ever.

He moans and dips his head to my shoulder, tensing with every aftershock that rumbles through my body.

The last of the spasms leave me boneless on the bed, and I suddenly break into a fit of giggles.

Ryan lifts his head and cocks an amused brow at me, his eyes sleepy and satisfied. "You found my performance amusing, Ms. Sunderwell?"

"No," I gasp, trying to catch my breath. My lungs are still heaving despite every other muscle and organ in my body being turned to happy, satisfied goo. "I'm trying to imagine a dildo doing *that* for a woman."

He huffs out a laugh and shifts so that he's not in danger of crushing me before pulling me close. His heart drums steady and strong against my ear, and I cuddle closer.

This afterglow stuff *rocks*.

"I think you have sex toys beat," I tell him.

"You most *definitely* have sex toys beat." He strokes my back and presses a kiss to my head. "Thank you for letting me be your first time."

"Thank *you* for being my first time." I pause, because

the Cassie of two weeks ago wouldn't have had the bravery to say everything else I want to say. But I don't want to be the Cassie of two weeks ago.

I want to be the Cassie of today.

"I'm glad I waited for you," I whisper.

His arms tighten around me, and one big hand cups my breast. "Me too," he whispers back. "Me too."

TWENTY-TWO

Ryan

LIKE MOST MORNINGS, I wake up with a thirty-pound raccoon asleep on my head and a crick in my neck from being pushed off my pillow in the middle of the night.

But this morning, I'm too ridiculously, outrageously, obnoxiously happy to care.

I float into consciousness with a smile on my face, a grin that gets bigger when I realize the warm weight on my chest is Cassie still snuggled beside me, her legs tangled in mine and her arm draped over my ribs. Memories from last night rush in, feeding the happy flames until I've got a bonfire roaring inside of me.

I've had my share of amazing nights with incredible women, but nothing like this.

Nothing like her.

I glance down, watching Cassie's eyelids flutter in her sleep, wondering how it's possible that she keeps getting prettier every time I look at her. Even now, with mascara smudged beneath her lashes and her hair in a wild tangle around her face, I could stare at her for hours.

But unfortunately the cranky bastard waking up on my head with a grumpy clacking sound has a limited tolerance for lolling about in bed. At least not until I've fetched his breakfast first.

"Five more minutes," I whisper, brushing George's paw away from my forehead.

He chitters in response and transfers his attention to my nose, squeezing the tip before trying to dart a digit into my nostril, something he knows drives me up the fucking wall.

"No, George," Cassie murmurs sleepily. "You can pick your friends and you can pick your nose, but you can't pick your friend's nose."

George gurgles in surprise—apparently only just realizing we're not alone in bed—and rolls off the pillow, landing on the floor with a *thunk* and squeak.

Cassie props up on her arms, eyes wide. "Oh no, is he okay?"

"He's fine," I say, grinning as George croaks irritably from the floor, making it clear he would disagree with that statement. "He's like a cat. He always lands on his feet. Or his ass. But considering the size of his rear end, that's a pretty soft place to land."

Cassie giggles. "I was wondering about that. I did a little Googling, and I don't think raccoons are supposed to be quite so…fluffy."

George croaks again and we both burst out laughing.

"I know," I say, still grinning so hard the muscle in my jaw is starting to ache. "The vet is always on me to put him on a diet, but if I cut portion size at home, he just goes looking for more food in the nearest dumpster. I should probably take him on longer walks. Or get him back on his tricycle."

"No way." She pulls on her glasses while she narrows her eyes at me. "You're messing with me. George can't ride a tricycle."

"George can ride a tricycle," I say, lifting two fingers in the air when she puckers her lips doubtfully in response. "Scout's honor. I modified Blake's old trike with a longer handle for him. We can take him out for a ride later if you want." I curl an arm around her waist, pulling her soft, warm body closer, wishing she hadn't pulled my tee shirt on before we drifted off last night. The only thing better than waking up with Cassie in my bed would be waking up with Cassie *naked* in my bed. "I mean, assuming you're up for spending more time with us."

Her lips curve in a shy smile. "Yeah. I would like that. I had a good time with you last night."

"I had a wonderful time with you last night," I say, letting my hand drift down to cup her ass through the tee shirt fabric. "Best night ever."

Her grin stretches to take up more real estate on her pretty face. "Whatever. I bet you say that to all the girls."

I shake my head, voice serious as a heart attack as I promise, "No. I don't."

"No?" she whispers, leaning in closer. "Cross your heart and hope to die?"

"Cross my heart and hope to die," I say, threading my fingers into her hair. I'm seconds away from a good morning kiss when George leaps onto the end of the bed with a hiss that's downright menacing.

Cassie jumps away from me, clutching the sheets to her chest while I glare down at my sorry excuse for a wingman. "No, George. Mind your manners. I'll get your breakfast in a minute."

At the word "breakfast," George's ears perk up and Cassie laughs. "I hear you, George. I'm pretty hungry myself."

I'm feeling empty too, I realize. "We never ate dinner last night, did we?"

Cassie shakes her head, her eyes dancing as she says, "No. We were too busy with other things."

I grin. "We were, weren't we? Way more fun than dinner."

"Way more fun," she says, laughing as her stomach lets out a long, gurgling growl. "But I could go for an energy boost."

"We definitely need to keep your energy up," I agree, tossing off the covers and swinging my feet to the floor. "So I can help you use it up again later."

"Sounds perfect." Her lips press together for a beat before she says in a rush, "Thank you for making my first time so perfect. It was better than I ever imagined it could be and I know that's all because of you."

I lean in, hands braced on the mattress. "Not true. It takes two, Sunderwell. Chemistry isn't a solo operation."

She winces. "That reminds me… I should head home and get dressed for work. I'm helping out in the lab while half the staff are home hiding from the press."

"Can't you play hooky? I've got the day off and nothing to do but make you a big breakfast and spoil you rotten."

"I think you already did that last night," she says, her cheeks flushing pink.

"That wasn't spoiling you, that was my pure and complete pleasure," I say, voice going husky as I recall how hot it was to have my mouth between her legs, tasting her sweet, salty heat, making her come for me.

She blushes even brighter red in response and it's so

cute I can't resist pressing a kiss to her dimple, a display of affection that summons another outraged squawk from the end of the bed.

"Fine, fine," I grumble, winking at Cassie as I pull away. "Hold that thought. I'll be back with breakfast in bed and no obnoxious fur baby. If I can't convince you to stay, at least let me feed you before you go."

"I could probably be convinced to stay." She watches me pull on a pair of pajama pants and cross to grab a shirt from the bureau with obvious appreciation, making me wish George had stayed out raising hell last night instead of coming home like a good trash panda. The look in Cassie's eyes makes me want to take clothes *off*, not put them on. "If you'll help me with some brainstorming in between fun stuff. I want to get a list of app ideas off to my virtual assistant in Bangkok by tonight. That way he can start coding the framework that I'll dress up with all the pretty stuff later."

I nod as I back toward the door, heading toward the sound of George banging his silver bowl on the floor in cacophonous objection to my lollygagging. "Totally. Sounds like fun. You helped me with my art, now I can help you with yours."

She beams at me. "Yeah. It is like art. Just art with numbers instead of a blowtorch."

George howls like he's being slowly disemboweled and Cassie laughs and slides out of bed, making shooing motions with her hands. "Go. Feed him. I'll come make coffee. I'm too excited about my day off to stay in bed."

I'm sad about her not staying in bed, but not for long. The sight of Cassie padding around my kitchen in nothing but a tee shirt that barely skims the top of her thighs is not something I'm going to complain about.

Thirty minutes later, she slides onto a stool beside me

at the kitchen counter, grabbing a fork and tucking into the eggs and bacon I whipped up in the cast iron skillet. She gives a happy moan. "Oh, man. I don't think breakfast has ever tasted so good."

"It's the cast iron skillet," I say around a bite of sinfully good smoked bacon. "And starvation. That's part of my game plan. Make sure you're so hungry anything I feed you will taste restaurant quality."

Her eyes dance. "Speaking of restaurants... Since we have the whole day, I was thinking maybe we could go for a bike ride together first, before we take George for his. I mean, it doesn't seem right to have eggs and bacon without a cinnamon roll."

I grin. "I like the way you think, Sunderwell." I lean in, bringing my lips a whisper away from hers. "I like the way you kiss even more."

"Ditto." She kisses me, slow and sexy, her tongue teasing against mine, confirming that everything is indeed better with bacon. Even smoking hot kisses.

After breakfast, I dress and take George out for a brief weed of the garden while Cassie runs back to her place to shower and call into the office to announce that she'll be working remotely. While I'm watering the cucumbers, I check in with the town InstaChat page to see if there have been any new developments only to find the gossip mill running wild. News of Cassie's conversation with the sheriff has gotten out and the warring camps are escalating the conflict to outright warfare.

One look at Cassie's face as she wheels her bike down her drive makes it clear she's seen it, too.

"I shouldn't have looked," she says, lips turned down hard at the edges. "I can't believe anyone thinks Savannah or I had anything to do with the fire or trashing the square or anything else. We would never put people at risk. Or intentionally damage the company she worked so hard to build."

"I know that," I say, without the slightest shred of doubt. Last night wasn't just sexy as hell, it was also intimate, revealing. Cassie dropped her walls and let me in, revealing the pure sweetness at the heart of her. She isn't capable of the kind of deception people are accusing her of, which is probably why this is so hard for her to understand. "People see the world as they are, not as *you* are, you know? It's not your fault they're so eager to see the worst in others, even when it's not there."

She frowns, blinking beneath her furrowed brows. "You're right, but it still makes me sad. I didn't realize there were this many bitter people in Happy Cat. They should change the name to Cynical Cat."

"Pessimistic Cat, maybe?"

She wrinkles her nose. "Nah, Cranky Badger. Do away with the cat part altogether."

I smile. "I think that's redundant. Aren't badgers always cranky?"

"I don't know, I'm not on intimate terms with many badgers." She cocks her head, shifting her attention to George, who is washing baby tomatoes he stole from the Honey Gold vine. We keep a water dish outside for just this reason. "What about you, George? Do you know many badgers?"

George pops a tomato in his mouth and chews, seeming to consider the question. Cassie smiles in response. "I wish he could talk. I have a feeling all the stuff milling around in his head would blow our minds."

"I'm not so sure. I think he's mostly thinking about what he just ate, what he's currently eating, or when he's going to eat again."

"To be fair, that's probably also true of half the people

in this town," she says, grinning guiltily as she props her arms on her handlebars. "Including me. I don't care if I'm persona non grata around here. I still want cinnamon rolls. And more coffee." She taps her new cup holder, the one I installed for her the day after our first date. "Thanks for this, by the way. You're the best."

"You're welcome." I grin. "Let's head out. I'm done here." I shut off the hose and turn to her, wiping my damp hands on my jeans. "But I think we should make a promise to each other—no checking InstaChat or email until tomorrow morning."

She stands up straight, pressing her lips together in a determined line. "You're right. No need to let gossip spoil the day. And who knows, maybe by then they will have moved on to something else."

Not likely, I think, but I keep the pessimistic thought to myself. Today isn't a day for dwelling on small-minded people or law-enforcement officials more concerned with making convenient connections than the right ones. Today is for enjoying the company of a woman who is quickly becoming one of my favorite people.

By the time we get back from our bike ride and coffee treat, we're feeling no pain, too high on sugar, caffeine, and last night's orgasm hangover to give negative things an ounce of our attention. And then Cassie suggests a swim and a picnic down by the creek and the day gets even better.

I have the pleasure of rubbing sunscreen on her fine back and watching her stretch out on a towel wearing nothing but a red, 1940s pin-up style one piece that is by far the sexiest piece of swimwear I've ever seen. We jot down notes for her app design in her notebook over chicken salad sandwiches and exchange war stories about our worst jobs ever—mine, cleaning the fry cooker at The

Little Chicken; hers, fetching coffee for a gaming designer who left water bottles full of urine all over his office for her to dispose of.

"And he made me recycle them," she says, gagging softly as we wander down to the water's edge. "So gross."

I wince in sympathy, but can't help but laugh. "I'm sorry. That's awful. Why are guys so gross?"

She squeezes my hand. "Not all guys. You're not gross. Not even a little bit."

I cut a glance her way. "You haven't seen the inside of my garage."

"I don't care about the inside of your garage," she says. "Just the inside of you. The heart and all that."

"All that is in fine working shape. Especially when you're around." I draw her close in the chilly spring-fed creek, warm her up with a kiss, and drift off for a nap an hour later with her lying on my chest in the summer sun, certain life doesn't get much better than this.

It's an idle thought, but when I wake up, it's still drumming softly inside my head.

Life doesn't get much better than this...

Much better than someone who makes you laugh and makes you think and makes you feel like everything is right with the world because she's there beside you.

The suspicion that I'm in deeper than I would have imagined possible after a few dates teases at the back of my mind, becoming something close to a certainty. And then Cassie and I take George for his tricycle ride and she laughs all the way down to the end of our road and back, that gorgeous, free and easy laugh only the people she trusts get to hear, and I'm going, going...

"But he needs a helmet," Cassie says, beaming at my ridiculous raccoon as he picks up speed, chasing a leaf down the blacktop. "Got to protect that big beautiful brain of his. I'll order one tonight. Two day delivery."

Gone.

I'm gone.

She's worried about my fur rascal's brain and she's already got my heart in her hands.

I stop, turning to her in the sunset light, memorizing the way she's smiling at me, so wide open and fearless it takes my breath away. I want to remember every second of this, of the moment I realized I'm in love with the girl next door. She returns my lingering look, the softness in her eyes making me hope she feels it too, how close we are to something incredible.

Close, and getting closer with every passing day.

And now, hopefully, with every passing night.

"Stay over again?" I ask, taking her hand. "I promise to feed you this time before I have my way with you."

She traps her lip between her teeth as she nods. "Yes, but I have a special request, if that's okay?"

I reach out, tucking a wisp of hair behind her ear. "Of course. Anything your stomach desires. I've got chicken and pork chops in the fridge that I can throw on the grill. Or if you're in the mood for vegetarian, I can grab a few things from the garden and—"

"Not that kind of special request," she says. "Though any and all of that sounds amazing, I just... I thought maybe..." Breath rushing out, she reaches into her purse, whipping out a plastic box with a hot pink dildo inside. "Maybe you could teach me what to do with this? I mean, I have a basic idea, but..."

My brows lift. "Well, I would. But I confess I've never used one."

"You haven't?" She blinks and a second later rolls her eyes. "Oh. Right. Why would you? You have a perfectly good…" She waves a hand in the general direction of my cock, making me laugh.

"I do," I say. "But it doesn't seem that complicated. I'm pretty sure we can figure it out."

She arches a brow. "Yeah? You think? If we put our heads together?"

"And all our other parts." I gather her into my arms, letting my hands slide down the small of her back to cup her bottom through her shorts. "Thanks for asking me. I'd be honored to help you figure out what you like."

Her palms smooth up my chest. "I like you."

"I like you too. So much." I lean down, capturing her mouth for a slow, sultry kiss I wish never had to end.

TWENTY-THREE

*From the texts of Cassie Sunderwell and
Savannah Sunderwell*

Savannah: I'm going to put the company up for sale. It's time. If the press gets any worse I'm going to have to pay someone to take it off my hands.

Cassie: You are not putting it up for sale. It's going to be fine. There's no such thing as bad publicity.

Savannah: Not true. Being accused of trying to burn down your own factory is definitely bad. All bad. I'm done, Cassie. I don't have the energy to defend myself, and I hate that you've been dragged into this mess.

Cassie: It's not a mess. It's just a rough patch. Seriously. Relax, go eat some scones, and let me take care of this. All will be well.

Savannah: Did you finally take up meditating?

Cassie: Nope.

Savannah: Is Olivia dosing you with her Valerian root tea? The one that puts three-hundred-pound men in an insta-coma?

Cassie: Nope. No tea. I prefer coffee; you know that.

Savannah: Then why are you suddenly so Zenned out? Because the big sister I know would not…
Oh…
I get it.
You're riding the post-orgasm train to Relaxation Station. Aren't you?!

Cassie: There could be some validity to that statement…

Savannah: OH MY GOD YOU DID IT!! YOU FINALLY LOST YOUR V CARD! I'M SO PROUD AND HAPPY FOR YOU!

Cassie: LOL. Stop. It's not like I cured cancer. No need for all the caps.

Savannah: YES THERE IS!! THIS WAS A BIG STEP FOR YOU! BUT YOU DID IT! YAY!!!! GO YOU!!! GO FUCK WIN!!!

Cassie: One more all caps sentence and I'm turning off my phone.

Savannah: Okay, okay. But you have to tell me more! I want to know everything! Was it amazing? Is sex your new favorite toy? Do you have waking dreams about his penis because it's the best penis in the world and all you want to do is be naked with it all day long?

Cassie: Yes, it was amazing. Yes, it's my favorite toy. And yes, I think about him all the time, but not just that part of him. All the parts of him. His big hands and his smile and the way he laughs and how sexy he looks cooking eggs in his boxer shorts and how gentle he is with George Cooney, even when he wakes up with a raccoon claw in his nose.
All of him. The whole package.

Savannah: Oh dear… I was afraid of this. The train is passing Relaxation Station and heading straight for Put a Ring on It Crossing.

Cassie: No! Omg, no way. A ring isn't anywhere on my radar. That's nuts, Savannah.

Savannah: Is it? Because what you just described sounds an awful lot like love to me.

Cassie: I just enjoy spending time with him. That's all. He makes me happy. Everything's better with him around. Me included. I'm more relaxed and productive than I've been in years. I'm going to have this app ready to launch in a month and then all you'll need to do is sit back and rake in the money.

Savannah: I wish I had even half your optimism.

Cassie: Maybe you should go get laid. It's pretty great. I highly recommend it.

Savannah: Ha! Nope. No more of that for me. I'm going to become a nun. Or maybe Mary Poppins, a woman too busy magically governessing the needy children of London to mess with passing fancies like sex and romance.

Cassie: But wasn't Mary Poppins dating that chimney sweep guy?

Savannah: No way! They were just friends, psycho. He may have had a crush, but Burt was not tapping the Poppins. She would have spanked him with her umbrella for trying.

Cassie: Well, maybe he liked a little spanky with his hanky panky.

Savannah: Who are you? And what have you done with my sister?

Cassie: I'm the alien pod person who's taken over her prefrontal cortex. You may call me Gorgon Rotovirus Twelve.

Savannah: You're so weird. Is Ryan aware of how weird you are?

Cassie: Yes. *smiley face emoji* He likes me that way. He likes me just the way I am.

Savannah: Wow. I just teared up a little. That's… That's beautiful, honey. I'm happy for you.

Cassie: Me too. I can't believe it, really. That this is my life. That I get to wake up to an amazing man who thinks I'm beautiful and sexy and smart and who loves being with me as much as I love being with him.

Savannah: You just used the L word twice. You realize that, right?

Cassie: Yeah. I do. And maybe…

Savannah: Maybe?

Cassie: Talk to you soon. I've got to go see a man about a stuffed squirrel. Gordon is making a firefighter outfit for me as a surprise for Ryan. It's his three-year anniversary of joining the department tonight.

Savannah: Ew. A squirrel? Seriously?

Cassie: Not ew. All of Gordon's squirrels are sourced from naturally deceased rodents. No animals are caged or treated cruelly in the creation of his masterpieces.

Savannah: Roadkill, Cassie. That means they're roadkill he picks up off the street. You are gifting your true love with roadkill. I beg you to stop and reconsider this choice.

Cassie: Nope. I have to follow my heart. And my heart says Ryan is going to treasure this thoughtful gift.

Savannah: All right. I guess you know best…

Cassie: That's the spirit. Now go find a sexy Englishman, drag him back to your bed, and don't set him free until he's put a smile on your face. Check in soon.

TWENTY-FOUR

Ryan

SLEEP IS IMPOSSIBLE. I'm coming off a grueling forty-eight on duty, during which we actually saw action every few hours—summer is fire season and it's hitting hard this year—but thirty minutes after I've collapsed onto my mattress I'm still lying awake staring at the ceiling.

My bed doesn't feel right.

There's something missing.

Someone missing.

I reach a hand out to the cool side of the mattress, wishing Cassie were here. This is the first time I've slept here alone since that first night. It's amazing how quickly I've grown addicted to the feel of her next to me, the smell of her shampoo lingering on the pillowcase, the comfort of knowing she's close enough to touch.

"But it's four in the morning," I mumble to George,

who is curled up at the foot of the bed, waiting for me to nod off so he can take up his preferred position nested in my hair. "If I go over there now, she'll think I'm crazy."

No sooner are the words out of my mouth than I hear a soft *tap-tap* on the window. I sit up, squinting in the moonlight cutting through the crack in the curtains, heart lifting even as I warn myself that it's probably just a tree limb hitting the glass. I swing out from under the covers and pad barefoot to the window in nothing but my boxer briefs, parting the curtains to reveal a wish come true.

Grinning so hard it makes my jaw ache a little, I unlock the window and pull it up. "Hello there, beautiful. I was just lying in bed, wishing you were here."

She smiles and the night is instantly brighter. "I heard your truck pull up. I tried to go back to sleep, but I was too excited. I wanted to be the first person to give you a happy firefighter-iversary present." She pulls what looks like a stuffed animal on a small black circular stand from behind her back and holds it up in the air. "For you."

It's a squirrel, I realize. One of Gordon's taxidermied squirrels, dressed in a tiny firefighter hat and coat and holding an…ax? Yes, an ax.

It's creepy.

And weird.

And oddly heroic looking, and I adore it nearly as much as I do this woman.

"Get in here," I murmur roughly. "I need to thank you properly for this amazing present."

She reaches up, and I grab her beneath the arms, drawing her inside as she walks her flip-flop-covered feet up the side of the house. "You really like it? You promise?"

"It's perfect." I set her on her feet, taking a quick beat

to close the window so the mosquitos won't get in, before I turn back to her, accepting the squirrel for closer inspection. I hold it up to the moonlight, admiring the detail on the costume. "It's the best firefighter-iversary present I've ever gotten."

It's also the *only* firefighter-iversary present I've ever gotten. I can't believe she remembered the date I mentioned offhand a few days ago.

"Oh, good." She clasps her hands together in a fist at her chest, drawing my attention to the thin white tank top and tiny striped sleep shorts she's wearing. "Savannah said you would think I was crazy."

I set her gift on top of the bureau and turn back to her, sliding my hands around her waist. "It is crazy. But I love it." I pull her against me, cock stirring as a closer inspection of her tank top reveals no bra beneath. "How can I ever thank you for your thoughtfulness?"

"You could take my shirt off," she teases, dimple popping. "I think you've already disposed of it with your eyes. Might as well get rid of it in real life."

"Have I told you how smart you are today?" I reach for the bottom of her top only for her to stop me with a hand on mine.

"No, you haven't. But you can—and take off my shirt as soon as we put George out. I believe in protecting the eyes of the innocent."

"And the obnoxious," I agree, starting for George. I scoop him up from the bottom of the bed, ignoring the grumbling sound he makes as I carry him across the room. "Get used to it, buddy. We'll let you in later if you're good." I set him on the floor in the hall and close the door.

And then I spin and jog back to Cassie, making her

laugh as I tackle her around the waist, sending us both tumbling onto the bed.

"If I didn't know better, I'd think you were happy to see me," she says, looping her arms around my neck.

"So happy." I nudge her thighs apart with my knees, settling my hips between her spread legs, loving the way her lashes flutter as my erection presses against her through our clothes. "Forty-eight is way too many hours to be away from you."

I kiss her and she hums her agreement against my lips, the vibration making her kiss taste even sweeter. Or maybe it's the fact that I've been away from her for two days straight, spending every second thinking about her, worrying about her, wishing I could be there for her as this ridiculous investigation pushes forward with Cassie as the prime suspect in the Sunshine Factory fire.

I've told Jessie and the sheriff and anyone who will listen that they're not going to find anything—Cassie is innocent—but it's clear from the look on their faces they think I'm blinded by lust.

But it's not lust. It's something more than that, something that makes my heart do a slow-motion dive into a vat of warm honey as I draw Cassie's shirt over her head, baring her gorgeous breasts.

"I've missed you," I murmur against her sinfully soft skin, kissing my way from one tight pink nipple to the other.

"Are you talking to me?" she asks, her breath already coming faster. "Or to them?"

"All three of you," I answer, circling her tip with my tongue, making her squirm beneath me. "You're all beautiful and sexy and fucking delicious." I pull her nipple into my mouth and suck. She digs her fingernails into the skin at the back of my neck and arches closer, moaning beneath her breath.

"God, Ryan," she whispers as I transfer my attention to her other nipple. "It feels better every time you touch me. How is that possible?"

Because I'm learning what she likes.

Because I'm memorizing every swiftly indrawn breath, sigh, and moan, enlisting them as my spies in my quest to make her come harder every time I take her to bed.

Because I'm falling in love with her, and love takes pleasure and makes it magic. Makes it sacred. Makes it something I don't know how I'm going to give up when she heads for home.

The thought is enough to plunk a giant rock down on the center of my chest. My throat goes tight and bitterness creeps in to mingle with the sweet taste of her so fresh on my tongue.

I pull back, gazing down at her, heart skipping a beat as I take in her dark hair spread over my pillow, her pale skin glowing in the moonlight, and that hungry look in her eyes I know is all for me.

"What's wrong?" She brushes tender fingers through my hair, guiding it away from my forehead.

I shake my head slightly, but then think better of it. I don't want to lie to her, and pretending I'm not getting crazy attached to her is a lie, plain and simple. "I can't stop thinking about that plane flight."

"Which one? Where are you going?"

"I'm not going anywhere," I say, lips curving on one side. "You are. And I don't like it, Sunderwell. Not one bit."

Her lips part softly as she nods. "Yeah. I know. Me either."

"I'm not ready to say goodbye, but I'm pretty sure long distance would kill me," I confess, rocking gently against her, nudging my cock against her clit. "I need to be with you like this. Need to feel you, taste you, be there to rub your shoulders after a hard day slaving over a keyboard."

"Yes," she says, her thumbs catching in the waist of my boxer briefs. "And inside me. I need you inside me. All the time."

"All the time," I echo, shoving the fabric down my thighs as Cassie slips out of her sleep shorts, revealing nothing beneath.

I groan at the sight, balls dragging heavily between my legs at the sight of her so pink and slick for me. Because she wants me as desperately as I want her. Because it's so right, so perfect, so—

I sink into her with a cry of relief and bliss tangled together as she calls my name. Just my name, but I hear so much more. As she wraps her legs around me and holds on tight, lifting into me as I glide in and out of her heat, I hear all the things we've both been too hesitant to say.

I hear that she wants me, needs me in her bed the way she needs air and water and late night video game bingeing when she's stressed. I hear that she's ready to do whatever it takes, to take a wild leap, to choose *us* because alone isn't going to work now that we know how good it is to be Cassie and Ryan.

For her to be mine.

For me to be hers.

"God, yes, baby, come for me, Cassie," I beg as I take her harder, faster, desperate to feel her tighten around me before I go. "I need to feel you. Oh, yes. Yes, baby."

She cries out, her head falling back as she tumbles over. I'm with her a second later, spinning out into that world where there's nothing but goodness and sweetness and the ineffable awesome that is being this close to my girl.

"I'll get my resume together tomorrow," I say as we're lying heavy in each other's arms, her cheek on my chest and my fingers skimming up and down the valley of her spine. "I'm not sure what the hiring situation is in San Francisco. But surely, with all the wildfires in California, they can use a few more good men."

Cassie's head pops up so fast it sends her hair flying into her face. "What?"

I brush her hair back, my heart skipping a beat, hoping I didn't take what she said in the heat of the moment the wrong way. "Being inside you all the time. That can't happen if I'm here and you're in San Francisco. So I figured I'd look into getting a job in your neck of the woods."

"You'd do that?" she asks in a hushed voice. "For me? Leave your brothers and your parents and everything you've ever known?"

"That's the thing," I say, swallowing hard as I debate whether or not to speak the words on the tip of my tongue. But fuck it. Fear never got me anywhere I want to be. "I've known all of those things. I've never known anything like this. Like you. And the way I feel when I'm with you."

Her bottom lip begins to tremble and a second later a tear slides down her cheek.

"I'm sorry," I say, hating myself for pushing too far, too fast. "I should have kept my mouth shut. It's too soon, I'm sorry, we don't have—"

"Hush." She covers my lips with her fingers as she swipes her tears away with the other hand. "No, it's not too soon. And no, you shouldn't have. I'm so glad you said something. I was afraid I was the only one."

"The only one who needs us to be in the same town?" I ask, relief taking the edge off my mini heart attack.

"The only one who's falling in love with you," she whispers.

My chest explodes. Or implodes. Or maybe that's just my heart doing the happy dance in a way I've never experienced before. Whatever it is that's happening to me, I don't want it to stop.

"I'm already there," I say, cupping her face in my hand.

Her eyes start to shine again, but she's smiling so big I know she's not sad. She's along for this ride with me, wherever it's going to take us.

"You don't have to move to San Francisco," she says. "I'm coming home. I already decided. Tonight. Three hours ago, in fact, when I was lying in bed feeling miserable because I couldn't imagine going back to a world where you're not right next door."

I'm about to ask her—How about a world where your house is *my* house?

I'm going to do it, ask her to move in with me on the spur of the moment, because that's what love makes you do, I guess, when the emergency alert on my phone goes off.

I curse softly and reach an arm for the bedside table. "Sorry. That's work. It must be something serious or they wouldn't be calling me back after less than two hours off." But when I pick up the phone, it isn't dispatch with instructions for where I need to show up and when.

It's the chief.

"You still awake?" Jessie asks.

"Yeah, I'm awake." I frown as I prop myself against the pillows. "What's up? Did that fire out by the highway flare up again? You need me back in?"

"No, nothing like that I..." She sighs. "I just thought you might still be up, and I wanted you to hear the latest development in the Sunderwell case from me."

I cut a quick glance Cassie's way to find her watching me with calm, clear eyes, making me think she can't hear Jessie's side of the conversation. I force a tight smile. "Sure, just a second, let me run get a pen."

"A pen?" Jessie's surprise echoes in my ear as I pull on pajama pants and head for the door. "You're not alone there, are you?"

"No, it's fine. You didn't wake me," I reply—*awkwardly*—because I'm terrible at lying. As soon as I'm on the other side of the kitchen, far enough away to be sure Cassie won't hear me, I add in a soft voice, "No, I'm not alone. Cassie's here."

Jessie sighs. "Then you should come talk to me. If it's gone that far with you two, you're going to need a friendly ear after you hear the latest."

A frown claws at my forehead. "Hear what? Cassie didn't start that fire, Jessie. I'm sure of it. I don't care what the new evidence is. It's wrong."

"It's inadmissible in court. It's not wrong," Jessie says, the compassion in her voice making my stomach clench with worry. "Just meet me at Dough on the Square in fifteen minutes, okay? I'll buy you a coffee and a donut and we can talk."

"I can't, I have company." I don't want to leave Cassie alone in my bed, especially not to go hear some bullshit "inadmissible evidence" that came from God knows what source.

Probably the real arsonist, trying to throw small-town law enforcement off his scent.

"I'm serious, Ryan. This is big. I wouldn't have called you right after your shift if it weren't. If you don't want to meet up, that's fine. I get it. But you're going to get an earful of this news sooner or later. If you'd like to have the chance to get out ahead of it, decide how you're going to handle the fallout when it comes, then I'll be at the donut shop in ten minutes."

I drag a hand through my hair, eyes squeezing shut. "Okay. Fine. I'll meet you in ten."

"See you then," Jessie says. "And for what it's worth, I'm sorry. I didn't want things to end up this way. I always thought Cassie and her sister were good people."

They are good people, I want to shout, but instead I tell Jessie I'll see her soon and end the call.

I'm in love with Cassie. I've seen every corner of her heart and I know she's incapable of arson. But me shouting "she's innocent" isn't going to help put this behind us. The best thing I can do for Cassie is to go see Jessie, take a look at this bullshit evidence, and convince the chief they're sniffing down the wrong trail.

I return to the bedroom to find George has let himself in through the now open door and is propped on my pillow next to Cassie, eating something gripped between his paws that's hard to make out in the dim light.

"No eating in bed, Cooney." I keep my tone light so Cassie won't worry. "You know the rules."

"But he brought me a present," Cassie says, laughter in her voice as she holds up something on a stick.

I flick on the closet light, laughing as I see the penis lollipop she's holding delicately between two fingers.

"It's official then," I say. "He loves you too."

George chitters in response, making Cassie giggle.

She's so happy, and hell if I'm going to let anything take that away. Jaw set, I tell Cassie I forgot something down at the station and will be right back. Then I dress and hurry out the door, ready to battle the powers that be until they back off the woman I love.

TWENTY-FIVE

Cassie

"CHERRY, LIME..." I take another lick of the pop, eyes narrowing as I try to pinpoint the mystery ingredient. "Cilantro?"

George shoots me a "you've gotta be kidding" look, grabbing another grape off his furry belly before returning his attention to *The Cat Whisperer*. Just as Ryan promised, my furry friend is rapt and giving me no guff.

But George has clearly accepted me as his own, as evidenced by the thoughtful gift dissolving on my tongue. It actually isn't half bad, considering its several years old and spent at least part of a night in a trashcan.

"But it was wrapped in plastic." I hold the partially melted peen up for perusal. "So I'm probably not going die, right?"

George clucks back at me, and I smile. If someone had told me a month ago that I'd soon be relaxing in the bed of a man I'm madly in love with, chatting with his pet raccoon, and plotting my cross-country move from San Francisco to Happy Cat, I would have said they were looney in the toons.

But love is crazy, I guess.

The best kind of crazy.

I'm sure Savannah is going to think I'm nuts at first too, but she'll be glad to have me home. I do the math, figuring out what time it is in the UK and decide to give my sister a call. Something like this isn't the kind of news that should be delivered via text message.

I lean over, fumbling for my pajama shorts on the floor and tugging my cell from the back pocket only to yip in surprise and drop the phone back onto the carpet when it begins to ring.

George bleats disapprovingly as I plop my feet off the bed. "I know, I know. It's probably your dad, calling to make sure we're getting along all right."

But when I flip the screen over, it isn't Ryan's number. It's from an area code I don't recognize. My first thought is that it must be a robo-call, but the spam centers usually have better timing, and a call at five in the morning is odd enough I feel compelled to answer.

I hit the answer button and bring the phone to my ear. "Hello?"

"Cassandra?" The voice is garbled, robotic, and instantly sends gooseflesh rippling across my skin.

"Who is this?" I ask, my heart beating fast in my throat.

"A friend. Or an enemy, depending on how you play your cards," the voice says, pushing on before I can tell him I'm not playing games, not with him or any of the other people trying to shut down my sister's company. That *has* to be what this is about. "Pay close attention,

Cassandra. I'm prepared to give the police everything they need to pin the fire at Sunshine Toys on you and your sister."

"Bullshit," I snap, my hands beginning to shake. "You don't have evidence because Savannah and I had nothing to do with the fire."

"So you say. But who are the police going to believe? Two town rejects who never fit in around here in the first place? Or evidence with your fingerprints all over it and eyewitnesses willing to testify that they saw you coming in and out of the factory in the early morning the day of the fire?"

"Those people would be lying and my fingerprints are all over everything at the factory because I *work* there, genius. I—"

"I'm not interested in arguing. You're in over your head and the only way out is to play nice, sweetheart. If you want to stay out of jail, you'll meet me at the factory in thirty minutes to discuss terms. Come alone and don't tell anyone about this call. If you do, I'll know, and I pull the trigger. Once I set the dominos to falling, life as you know it is over, Cassie. Forever. So hurry up and get dressed. I'll be waiting."

There's a sharp click as the call disconnects. I curse, jaw clenching tight, and toss the phone on the bed.

George shoots me a curious look as I drive a hand into my hair and make a fist.

"I don't know," I mumble, pacing toward the window and then back to the bed, pulse pounding. "He doesn't have any evidence—there's no way he could—but he's right. If people are willing to lie and this asshole has doctored something to make it look like I'm behind this…"

I bite down hard on my lip. I want to call Ryan so much it's all I can do to keep from diving for the phone.

But the man said he would know.

He also told me to get dressed…

A shiver racing up my spine, I hurry to the window and tug the curtains closed. My arms are shaking so badly it takes three tries to get them all the way shut.

"It's the butt crack of dawn," I mumble. "Maybe he just assumed I was in pajamas and would need to change."

But my racing heart isn't buying that and neither is George, who rolls onto his feet, fussing as I grab a pair of Ryan's track pants from his bottom drawer. "I know it's a dumb idea," I say, "but I have to go. I don't have a choice."

George whine-growls.

"I'll be careful, I promise."

He plops down on his bottom in the middle of the bed, looking lost.

I can empathize…

Silently assuring myself that the factory is so close to downtown that all I'll have to do is call for help if things get creepy, I pull the pants on, rolling them up at the waist and tugging the drawstring tight. I pair them with a black tee shirt that proclaims *Wild Hog Wild and Proud of It* across the front and slip into the flip-flops I wore across the grass to Ryan's place.

If I'm going to get to the factory in ten minutes, I'll have to hurry. There isn't time to run home and change.

Shit. I picked up a nail in my car tire yesterday and haven't fixed the flat yet. I'll have to ride my bike. Even pedaling at top speed and taking the shortcut, I'll be cutting it close.

But it's fine. I'll just ride in quietly in my black

clothes, figure out who this asshole is, and get home as fast as possible.

If I'm lucky, I'll be back in bed before Ryan, with the Sunshine Toys disaster handled and the future looking nothing but bright.

But as I pump hard through the eerie quiet of early morning, the sun still so low the sky is the color of an ugly bruise, every cell in my body screams that I'm making a mistake.

A scary, potentially profound mistake.

TWENTY-SIX

Ryan

JESSIE'S WAITING for me in front of the donut shop, her hands tucked into the pockets of her HCFD windbreaker, a nod to the breezy morning. It's cool now, but in another hour or two, once the summer sun peeks over the horizon, it's going to warm up fast. I make a mental note to turn the air conditioning on before I crawl back in bed with Cassie.

Because I *will* be getting back in bed with Cassie.

Whatever Jessie has to share with me, it's not going to change my mind about a future with the woman I love.

"Step around back for a second?" Jessie nods toward the alley between Dough on the Square Donuts and the mortuary next door.

I smile. "Going full cloak and dagger?"

Jessie doesn't smile back. "Just don't want to risk anyone else getting an earful of this. I probably shouldn't be sharing it with you, but…" She shrugs, but I have no trouble filling in the mental blanks.

I'm like a kid brother to her. Jessie was on the team that pulled me out of the fire that almost claimed my life via a massive case of smoke inhalation and has had a soft spot for me ever since. She's my boss, yes, but she's also my mentor and friend. She's also a rule-follower, and the fact that she's willing to bend the rules for this makes my stomach clench as I nod and follow her around to the side of the building.

"Sometimes this feels like a warning I'm choosing to ignore." She motions to the ramp leading up to the mortuary's side entrance mere feet from the bakery. "The consequences of donuts and all."

I grunt in agreement. "Yeah, I think I'll skip the cruller today."

"You're a better man than I am. Life's too short to skip the jelly donut. Especially if it's raspberry jelly."

I cross my arms, studying Jessie's face in the glow of the streetlight spilling into the alley. "Life's too short not to be loyal to the people you care about too. I feel like a traitor being here."

"I know. I'm sorry about that. But…" She pulls her phone from her pocket and swipes, punching in the code to unlock the screen. "Have a listen for yourself."

She taps a voice memo and a familiar voice crackles through the air. It's not a great connection on the recording, but I know it's Cassie the second she says, "You're going to be okay. Better than okay. You're going to come out the other side of this stronger than ever. No doubt in my mind."

The person on the other end of the line sobs and Cassie makes a soft, clucking sound of sympathy. When she speaks again, her words are thick with emotion. "Oh, sweetheart, I'm so sorry. I hate that he hurt you. I want to fly down there right now, wrap my hands around his lying, cheating, sheep-abusing neck and strangle him."

"It *is* sheep abuse," Savannah wails. "He said they were in love, but a sheep doesn't have feelings. Not like that. A sheep can't choose, Cassie. A sheep is just a sheep!"

"I know, I know." Cassie growls. "Argh. That creep should be in jail."

Savannah's next sob ends in a bitter laugh. "Yeah, right. Steve's still a pillar of the community. No one wants to believe it. *I'm* the deviant who owns a sex toy factory. A sucky sex toy factory that's probably going to be out of business by the end of the year."

"That's not true," Cassie says. "Things are going well, you said so yourself just last week."

"Not well enough and I'm too tired to fix it now. I've lost my will to care about orgasms. I hate orgasms. I hate sex. And I hate sheep. And I hate half the people in this town for loving Steve so much. They don't even believe me. I hate everything."

Cassie makes hushing noises for a long beat and Jessie and I exchange uncomfortable looks. It feels wrong to be eavesdropping on a private conversation, but I'm assuming we're getting close to the allegedly incriminating part, a hunch confirmed with Savannah sobs, "I just want to run away, Cass. Torch my life, run away, and let it burn."

I frown. If this is the evidence, they're reaching hard for it. Savannah's clearly talking figuratively, not literally. I'm about to say as much when Cassie's voice pipes up again.

"And if it comes to that, I'll help you, okay? But let me come down there and fill in for you first. You can take a trip, and I'll mind the factory while you're gone. That way you can take time to heal before you decide what you really want to do."

"Burn it down," Savannah mumbles. "Burn it all down."

"Okay, okay," Cassie soothes. "We'll figure it out. Just don't do anything crazy before I get there to help, okay?"

Jessie taps the end button. "There's more, but that's the relevant part."

"It's a stretch, chief," I say, shaking my head. But I can't deny there's a whisper of doubt in my head that wasn't there before. I'm still ninety percent sure this is an innocent conversation taken out of context, but…

"It is," Jessie agrees. "And like I said on the phone, it's inadmissible in court. But the fingerprints they pulled from the chemical drums Sheriff Briggs found at the dump yesterday are going to be enough to put Cassie in a tough spot."

"What chemical drums?" I ask, propping my hands low on my hips.

"The sheriff got an anonymous tip from a concerned citizen, probably the same one who sent him this conversation."

"How did they get their hands on that conversation, by the way?" I ask, jabbing a finger at Jessie's phone. "That was clearly private."

Jessie's shoulders rise and fall. "I don't know. Maybe someone was recording outgoing calls from the factory. Or maybe someone suspected Savannah was on the verge of doing something dangerous and tapped her phone."

"Sketchy. And not someone I'm inclined to believe. If they're so righteous and concerned, why not come out of the shadows?"

Before Jessie can answer, the wailing of sirens echoes

through the square. We turn in time to see a fire truck rush by and we hurry out of the alley.

"I'll call dispatch, see what's up," Jessie says, but I already know what's up.

Or what's been lit up.

The smoke rising from the end of Main Street could be coming from the post office or the taxidermy shop, but I instinctively know it's not. It's Sunshine Toys.

On fire.

Again.

TWENTY-SEVEN

Cassie

I'M AN IDIOT.

I noticed the back door felt warm to the touch, but I went in anyway. I pushed inside, got doused with a rush of foul-smelling liquid someone must have propped above the door, and now I'm trapped in a smoke-filled room. Something's on fire in the staff locker room and the door I came in through is stuck tight.

I haul on the handle, throwing my full weight into it, but it doesn't budge and soon I'm coughing too hard to stand up straight.

I fall to my knees, sucking in deep breaths. The air is cleaner down here.

After a few moments my head clears, and I start toward the staff bathrooms on my hands and knees. There's a window in the women's bathroom. It's high and tight, but there's a chance I can get through it. Even if I can't, I can at least soak my clothes with water and huddle in the far stall until the cavalry arrives.

The fire department will be here soon, before this fire has the chance to become too dangerous.

I'm sure that's what whoever started it was counting on.

Someone started this fire, I realize in a burst of clarity. Someone started this fire and then summoned me here so I'd be right in the middle of it when Happy Cat's finest showed up to put it out.

I'm getting angry—*really* angry—and then I push through the door to the bathroom and look up to see a pair of shoes disappearing through the open window.

They're Italian loafers.

Italian *fucking* loafers.

I know those loafers. Savannah bought those loafers the last time she came to see me in San Francisco.

As a present.

For the sheep-fucker.

"Steve!" His name emerges as a croak from my smoke-raw throat and my demands for him to get his ass back here and confess to what he's done end in a coughing fit. I shut the bathroom door behind me, but the smoke is still getting in somehow.

A vent? The ceiling?

I have no idea, but by the time I crawl-cough down the aisle of toilets to the window, I'm dizzy and my lungs feel like they've been clawed at from the inside. I stand, reaching for the window ledge, but I'm too short. I can barely curl my fingers around it and there's no way I'm going to have the strength to pull myself up. Even a rock-climbing badass my height would struggle with this one, and I am no kind of badass.

I'm an idiot. A fool covered in foul-smelling funk,

coughing her head off on the floor of a bathroom, reduced to praying that someone will come save her before it's too late.

My gut says Steve didn't intend to kill me—just frame me good and proper—but that might not matter.

I could die here, I realize, head spinning as I sag against the wall, tears rising in my eyes. I could die and Ryan will never know why I left his bed or how I came to be here. He might even assume I really am behind all this and that…

Well, that is maybe the saddest thing ever.

My chest goes tight, so tight, and raw. And then my head is spinning and I'm sliding onto the white tile for a nap, visions of Steve being stabbed with a hundred tiny pitchforks while demon sheep tap dance on his spine spinning through my head.

Then there's nothing.

It's all smoke and fog and a buzzing sound, high and insistent in my ears.

AND THEN SUDDENLY I'M waking up on a gurney outside under a pale blue morning sky with an oxygen mask covering my nose and mouth and Ryan staring down at me with a mixture of worry, pain, and disgust that breaks my heart.

Broken—crash, bam.

Right in two.

TWENTY-EIGHT

Ryan

I HUNCH over the Wild Hog's bar, head pounding, heart aching, gut roiling.

Dual images keep flashing in my head.

One of Cassie, dousing lighter fluid all over the factory.

The other of her ashen face when Jojo pulled her out of the building.

"Pour me another," I order Jace.

He scowls at me, slams both hands on the bar, and leans across it until he's right in my face. "I cannot serve you liquor until eleven. I *told* you that."

He also filled my first glass with our grandmother's lemonade, which would probably get him shut down if anyone knew what was in it.

I don't give two shits right now.

"She set the fire, Jace." The words are hollow, and

they taste like burnt black licorice and raccoon shit. "She set the fucking fire."

I still can't believe it, but between that phone call recording, everything that's gone wrong for Sunshine the last two weeks, and then *finding her there*, when she was supposed to be *at my house*, what am I supposed to think?

Something smacks the back of my head, and I realize it was my brother's hand. "If you believe that," Jace growls, low and tight, "then you don't deserve her."

"Whatever he's having, I want something different." Blake slides onto the stool next to me. "And can I order a shower for him? He smells like smoky ass."

Jace hooks a thumb toward the john. "If you can get him in there, you can give him a shower in the sink."

The Wild Hog's pretty much deserted this early in the day, with just one small group of farmers back at the arcade games. Most of the town's gawking at the carnage over at the Sunshine factory—happy name for a miserable place—or they're busy telling the sheriff all the ways they knew Cassie wasn't right in the head from the moment she got back.

Those Sunderwell girls were never really *one of us. So stuck up, with all the Hollywood attitude. We should've known they were deviants—not too far a stretch from selling perverted toys to setting fires.*

I thought they were wrong, that it was small-town pettiness. But then, never in a million lifetimes would I have suspected Cassie would set fire to anything.

But maybe Jessie was right about the lengths family will go to for each other.

What wouldn't I do for one of my brothers?

I'd like to think I wouldn't push too far. But I also know Jace and Ginger. My brother will be a damn good father, and if Ginger does *anything* to put my niece or nephew in danger, or to keep the child from Jace, the line between right and wrong might get blurry.

Maybe it got blurry for Cassie too.

But setting a fire, putting innocent people and her own life in danger? It's a line I cannot stomach seeing crossed, not after everything I've been through in my life. Not after swearing to protect the people of this town, to give my life for them if necessary.

It's too fucking much.

Jace pushes a Coke across the bar to Blake. "You want to talk some sense into him, or should we take him out back and do it the old-fashioned way?"

"I got him."

"Good, because I can't afford to get arrested again." Jace jerks his head toward the kitchen. "I'll be in back. Holler if you need me."

"Nobody's gonna arrest you," I grumble. "They're too busy arresting an arsonist."

Jace flips me off before he disappears.

"Hey, man, how about we take a break from being a dick for two minutes." Blake's perpetual cheer is grating on my nerves, and Jace didn't refill my lemonade.

"I'm not being a dick. I'm being *broken*." Apparently one lemonade was enough on an empty stomach.

"No, you're not. You're being a chickenshit."

I try to shove his shoulder, and fall off my stool.

But Blake catches me.

He's my brother. That's what brothers do. But usually I'm the one doing the catching.

How much vodka was in that lemonade?

"I'm not a chickenshit," I protest while he puts me back into my seat.

"Then you're an asshole," Blake replies happily.

Always happy, that's Blake. He could bottle it and sell it as Moonshine. Happyshine. Sunshine.

Fuck.

"Not a hucking assfole either," I slur. When did the bar move onto a boat, and why is it rocking?

"Jesus, Ry. When's the last time you slept?"

I squint at the two Blakes. "Thursday? Had a shizzy bift. A biffy shitz. A—hell."

"A busy shift?" he suggests.

I point a finger at him and cock it. "Thassit."

"Gimme your keys, you idiot. We're going home."

"No. Not home. *She* was home. Not going home. Can't make me."

"Can and will. C'mon, big bro. You can thank me tomorrow."

"Ain't thank you for nothin'."

"You'll be thanking me for not recording this. Hey, Jace! Come get the door."

Are my lips numb? I think my lips are numb.

The world spins again, and I'm suddenly upside down with a shoulder in my gut. "Wha tha fuuuu…?"

"You might not be recording," Jace says, "but I sure as hell am."

"No more lemonade after a double shift," Blake grunts. "You know what *sugar* does to him."

I must be dying, because I swear Jace just laughed.

Jace doesn't laugh.

Now I get why.

I'll never laugh again either.

I close my eyes. There's Cassie.

Lighting the fire.

Pale and limp on Jojo's back.

Lighting the fire.

Lying seemingly lifeless outside the building.

Lighting the fire.

Coming to on the stretcher, those bewitching eyes lying to me.

"Oh my goddess, what are you doing?" Olivia's voice shrieks into the floaty area around my ears. "Are you going to drop him on his head?"

"Might be more effective than taking him home," Blake muses.

"You can't drop him on his head! We need him to help Cassie!"

"He's not in good enough shape to help George Cooney right now, let alone a human being."

"Put. Him. Down."

Is that really Olivia?

Whoever she is, she's persuasive. I'm suddenly back on the ground with my ass in a chair, mist spraying into my face. "Ow! Hey! What the hell?"

"It's an aromatherapy spritzer." Olivia gives the perfume bottle one more squirt in my direction. "It cures dumbness. And hangovers."

"It smells like burnt tar and cat spray." But the fog in my head is clearing. Whatever's in that shit is potent.

And effective.

"You need your chakras realigned," she declares.

"He needs to get over being scared," Blake replies.

I shoot him a *what the hell?* look.

He shrugs. "Love's a big fucking deal. And scary as hell. You want to go slow, go slow. But don't sabotage the one thing you've always wanted. You can't protect the world, Ry. Sometimes people get hurt. And that includes the people you care about. You can be afraid of it, but don't let fear stop you."

"I'm not afraid," I grunt.

"Dude, Jace is less terrified of being a father than you

are of admitting seeing Cassie on that stretcher almost killed you."

"A f-father?" Olivia's brows crinkle.

Jace grunts and gives a short nod, not looking at her.

Her lips part, and if I wasn't sleep-deprived and tipsy on more than just an adrenaline crash, I'd say she was hurt.

"Blake's right," Jace tells me. "You're being a chickenshit."

"I'm *not* scared," I insist.

"Then why didn't you stick around to listen to what she had to say?" Blake asks.

I offer him a middle finger. "I read people pretty damn well."

He snorts. "You shut the cover on that book before you got to Chapter One. C'mon. You can crash at my place for a few hours. And then we're calling Clint, and all three of us are going to kick your ass together."

"I'm protecting *you*," I tell them all. "Protecting you from an arsonist getting too close to this family."

"You're an idiot," Jace says.

Blake shakes his head. "You ever stop to think about why you've never had a steady girlfriend more than a few months? I used to think it was because you didn't want the responsibility of a relationship after all you did for us. But I don't think that's it anymore. Know what I think?"

"That you think too much?"

"That you're afraid you'll get a wife and kids and you won't be able to keep them safe. That you won't be able to be the hero every second of the day." He pauses, arching a brow. "Or maybe you're worried you'll have a kid who's just like you, who feels like he has to pick up your slack and worry all the time and he'll never give himself a moment's peace."

"You don't know what the fuck you're talking about."

The low-lit interior of the bar is in sharp focus now.

So's the clenching in my chest.

And the twist in my gut that says my brother has a fucking point.

Blake's green gaze doesn't waver as he shrugs. "Maybe I don't. But I also know it's not like you to abandon someone you care about who needs you. You should think about what's really going on here, brother."

What's *really going on* is that Cassie Sunderwell played me. Hard and ugly.

But…she was so excited about that gaming app she wanted to write.

Seemingly sincerely excited. Was that really just a ploy to ensure she'd have a strong defense when she lit up her sister's factory? And the way she blushed her face off, but kept trying to get comfortable with sex toys. And the way she brought a dildo to bed and trusted me to help her to figure out how to use it.

And the way she made my heart jolt fully awake for the first time in my life and how she nearly stopped it cold while she was lying unconscious on that stretcher and there was nothing I could do.

I'd been too late. Helpless.

In that second, I got a glimpse of what it would be like to live in a world without her, and it was…terrifying. A flat-out fucking nightmare.

Blake pinches his lips together and nods, as if he's reading my mind. And knowing he was right…the bastard.

"I know what else is going on," Olivia suddenly interjects with a frustrated huff. "Steve set the fire and nearly killed one of my favorite people in the process, that's what's going on."

I suck in a breath through my nose, and the acrid scent still lingering on my clothes taunts me. "What?"

"Steve set the fire," Olivia repeats slowly. "And if you don't listen to me and get on Team Cassie *right now*, I'm going to dunk your head in a toilet and call you terrible names that I have never called *anyone* in my entire life."

There's a giant, gaping hole opening in my heart, widening with every word. "Steve set the fire."

"Shocker," Blake says pleasantly.

"Cassie saw his shoes going out the window," Olivia insists. "But he's poker buddies with the sheriff. Savannah says that's why he didn't get charged with assault of a farm animal. Also, Cassie got a phone call from a creepy voice threatening to frame her and Savannah for all the bad stuff at the factory if she didn't meet him there. So that's what she did. She went to the factory, and she saw Steve's shoes going out the window. She was *framed*. And she needs you. And if you don't help her, I'll create an aromatherapy spritzer that will leave you impotent for life, O'Dell. And if you think I won't use my goddess-given powers for revenge, then you have another think coming, mister!"

Everything in my brain is buzzing. Everything in my chest is buzzing.

And none of it in a good way.

Because every last cell in my body recognizes the truth.

Blake's right. I never should've doubted Cassie.

And if Olivia's right—if Steve did this, then I have fucked up so badly I might never know true sunshine in my life. Not ever again.

"I'm a dumbass," I mutter.

Blake winks at me. "Happens to the best of us. You just took a long time getting around to your turn."

Cassie's never going to forgive me.

Hell, *I* wouldn't forgive me if I were her. But I have a more pressing matter to take care of than begging for her forgiveness.

I need to make sure she's safe. "Do you know where she is?" I ask Olivia.

"At the bakery. Maud's the only person in town the sheriff's afraid of."

I leap up off my seat on a new adrenaline high.

I've let her down too many times already.

This time, I'm going to get *something* right.

Her life might depend on it.

TWENTY-NINE

Cassie

"HERE, HONEY." Maud Hutchins sets another fresh blueberry cupcake with extra cream cheese icing on the table in front of me. "It's okay to have two on days like today."

"Or three," Gerald grumbles from the other side of the bakery's cheery—and abandoned—counter. Everyone's too busy milling around the farmers' market in the square, gossiping about my "latest" arson attempt to have time for cinnamon rolls and sugar cookies.

But Maud and Gerald have made it clear that I'm welcome here. Even Gerald, Sunshine Toy's most passionate detractor, believes I've been framed. Even Gerald, who thinks I'm part of a deviant conspiracy to steal decent women away from their husbands with battery-powered orgasms, is on my side.

But Ryan just…walked away.

He made sure I was alive, shook his head at me like I was the one who'd broken *his* heart, and. Walked. Away.

No looking back.

Tears rising in my eyes for the tenth time since I left the hospital, I dig into my cupcake with my already icing-sticky fork. Better enjoy sweet treats and my freedom while I have them.

By the end of the day, the sheriff could have a warrant for my arrest.

"Don't cry," Ruthie May says, patting my hand from across the table. "We're going to take care of this. Savannah's lawyer is the best in the state. You know that. That's how she got away from Steve with all her money still in her bank account."

"Deborah's a shark," Maud agrees. "She'll take care of you, honey."

"But she's not a criminal attorney." I sniff hard, refusing to start sobbing again. My lungs are strained after all the smoke inhalation, my throat raw, and my eyes itchy enough without adding tears to the mix. "She's just coming to chat as a favor to Savannah. I'll have to find someone else to represent me if I'm actually arrested." I press my lips together, throat working as I fight for control.

But the fact that the words "warrant for arrest" might soon apply to me is too much.

I'm a rule follower. A law-abiding nerd from way back. I've never had so much as a parking ticket. And now, thanks to Savannah's evil ex, I might be going to jail.

"And I don't even smoke," I whisper. "I'll have nothing to trade for protection in prison."

"You are not going to prison," Gerald says firmly. "I'll

wring a confession out of Steve with my bare hands before that happens."

I shift my gaze to the big man with the kind eyes and smile. "Thank you, Gerald. I appreciate your support."

"Of course," he says, looking flustered by my gratitude. "A fair fight is one thing. But when one side starts playing dirty, decent people have to stand up for what's right. I don't want to live in a town with a sex toy factory, but I want to live in a town where innocent women go to jail even less."

"You're a good man, honey," Maud says, her eyes shining. "I always knew you'd come around."

"Speaking of coming around," Ruthie May murmurs, nodding toward the picture window looking out onto the street. "Looks like someone's pulled his head out of his backside."

I turn to see Ryan—looking gorgeous in faded jeans and a tight red tee shirt—pushing in through the door to the bakery. Immediately my heart pumps faster for reasons having nothing to do with the cupcake-fueled sugar rush laying claim to my system.

I meet his eyes across the room, steeling myself against the stupid wish that we could go back to how things were a few hours ago.

He *left* me. Right when I needed him the most.

Fool me once, shame on you. Fool me twice…

His blue eyes are soft. Searching. And something that looks a lot like regret tightens his features as I double down on the resolve to be strong for *myself* this time.

"Can we talk? Maybe…outside?" he asks. "Please?"

"I don't think we have anything left to say to each other." The words hurt like ripping off a bandage. I thought heartbreak was bad when I was a teenager, but this is worse. So much worse.

"Cassie—"

"Please leave." It's killing me to stay strong, but when you discover the person you love doesn't care enough to be at your side through better or worse, the *only* thing to do is to get out while you can.

"I know you didn't set the fire," Ryan says.

I can't keep the bitterness out of my voice when I reply, "Oh, really? So you were just pretending like I did to protect me? Because you care so much?"

He hangs his head and rubs a hand over his jaw like he's feeling a fresh bruise, like I physically slapped him. "I wasn't thinking straight. Jessie had just played me this phone conversation between you and Savannah and—"

"What? What phone call? Jessie recorded my private calls?"

"What in the *hell* is this world coming to?" Gerald growls. "Last time I checked, this wasn't a surveillance state!"

Ryan holds a hand up. "Someone sent it to the sheriff, who shared it with Jessie. I don't know who, but I can guess." He sighs. "Olivia told me about you seeing Steve's shoes. He probably—"

"So you believe *Olivia*, but you couldn't even stay and talk to *me*?" Now I feel like I'm the one being slapped in the face.

Over and over. With a sock stuffed with a brick. Or concrete dildos.

"You need to leave." My voice is stronger this time, even though my heart is crumbling into pieces.

He's not the man I thought he was. The man I wanted to *believe* he was.

I almost hope the sheriff does come and arrest me.

There's no chance I'll fall in love with anyone in prison.

"Cassie, please, I—"

"The lady asked you nicely," Gerald says.

"More than nicely," Maud agrees.

"I think you best be gettin' on," Ruthie May chimes in. "I've always liked you, Ryan. Don't make me change my mind."

He opens his mouth like he's going to argue, but instead, he turns, shoulders drooped, and heads for the door.

I barely keep the sob in check until the bells stop jingling behind him.

"Aw, honey," Maud says.

Ruthie May squeezes my hand.

And Gerald quietly sets another muffin before me.

It's heartbreak medicine, and I'm going to need a lot more before I'm healed.

If I ever heal.

THIRTY

Ryan

I'M DONE LETTING Cassie down. I'm going to fix this. All of it.

Her being framed for trying to destroy Sunshine.

People judging her and Savannah because of Sunshine.

That broken look on her face when I told her about Jessie and Olivia and Steve.

I'll prove to her that she comes first for me, no matter what it takes. Starting with the sheriff.

I track him down outside the factory, where today's shift is still doing recon on the fire that took out the east wing. "Sheriff. Cassie didn't do this."

Briggs lifts an uninterested brow. "I think you're thinking with parts of you best left out of this discussion."

"She saw Steve—"

"She told me her story."

My jaw slips, because it's clear he thinks she's lying. "Have you talked to Steve yet?"

"Son, how I do my job is none of your damn business."

"I can't believe this." I shake my head. "You're believing a guy who fucked a sheep over Cassie? Just because she's running a sex toy factory?"

"I didn't find any evidence of a sheep being violated by Steve Bennington."

"Because the sheep didn't report it?" I scoff.

He ignores my sarcasm. "Steve's been an upstanding member of the community for years. A lot longer than this wart on our community has been here, that's for sure. Happy Cat ain't the place for a sex factory."

"That's not your call to make," I say, voice tight. "And you owe it to the entire *town* to get to the truth."

He puts a sympathetic hand on my shoulder. "Them Sunderwell girls really know how to screw a guy up good, don't they? But you'll be all right, son. Give it a few days, then come on over to the house. The missus wants you to meet our Geri Lynn. She's home from college, got her bachelors of fine arts and everything."

I shake his hand off.

If he won't investigate Steve, I'll have to do it for him.

I CALL my brothers for backup, and they meet me at my house with Olivia in tow. Olivia and Jace keep casting covert, longing glances at each other when the other isn't looking, and it's getting a little weird, but I have bigger issues to sort out than whatever's going on between them.

For once, I'm putting my problems first.

No, I'm putting *Cassie* first.

The way it should be.

"We need his shoes," Blake says. "If he was at the factory, they'll probably have the lighter fluid all over them."

"Accelerant," I mutter. "We don't know exactly what it was yet."

"How the fuck are we going to get his shoes?" Jace asks.

"I'll just go ask him to borrow them," Olivia says. "For a friend who's coming into town or something."

Jace looks at her. She glances at the family photo I have hanging over the couch, then stares down at her feet as she adds, "I can be persuasive. When I need to be."

"But you're his ex-wife's best friend," Jace points out.

"Exactly. He's used to—oh." Olivia's shoulders slump. "Right. He won't talk to me, let alone give me evidence. Of course he won't."

"Forget *asking* for his shoes." I pace my living room, past the metal raccoon faces I welded and hung on the wall for George, because the little scavenger has an ego. "We need to *take* them. Or something that proves he's behind this."

"They won't be admissible in court if you steal them," Blake points out.

All three of us look at him.

He grins. "What? I like crime shows."

George wanders into the room, fat and forlorn. He misses Cassie too.

I've ruined the best relationship my raccoon ever had.

I'm about to switch on *The Cat Whisperer* for him when a diabolical idea strikes.

The one thing George loves even more than *The Cat Whisperer*?

Scavenging.

I squat down next to him and bat away the gnawed-on butt plug he's carrying. "George, you want to see Cassie again?" I ask.

He cocks his head, but remains skeptical.

"She needs your help, buddy."

"You have seriously lost every last ounce of your shit," Jace says.

"Hold on, hear him out," Blake replies. "I want to see where this is going."

"You in?" I ask George. "Might be a little tricky getting you to grab something that's not shaped like a vibrator or a penis pop, but…"

"Oh, dear." Olivia sighs. "I have an idea where this is going."

Jace arches a brow her way, but she just shakes her head. "Never mind. You'll find out soon enough."

I smile. He will find out.

So will Steve, the asswipe arsonist.

And he's never going to see this one coming.

AN HOUR LATER, Blake, George, and I are creeping through the woods behind Steve's house. We left Jace behind because if we get caught he can't afford another run-in with the law. We left Olivia behind because she confessed she couldn't be trusted not to blast Steve with impotence spritz, and we're not out to physically damage him.

Even though he deserves it.

"This is insane," Blake says. He's smiling, though, and I almost work up a smile in return.

Almost.

"You ready, George?" I ask, setting him down at the edge of Steve's impeccably manicured lawn.

He chirps, bobbing a paw in the air.

I unhook his leash and point to the cans beside house. "Go on. Go find something good in the trash."

"Completely nuts," Blake adds with a bigger grin. "But you're right, my Google Fu proves there's no precedent on evidence obtained by trash panda."

"See? I think *brilliant* was the word you were looking for."

We hunch in the timber behind the brick ranch while George waddles across the yard until he reaches the trash cans beside the house. In three quick leaps, he's teetering on the smaller recycling can while he lifts the lid on the big trash can a sliver and dives in, leaving it to drop closed behind him.

"I can't believe you sleep with that," Blake mutters.

"He washes up before he gets in bed."

Something moves inside, behind one of the windows, and I drop flat against the ground.

"What's he doing home?" Blake whispers. "I thought he always spent Sundays at his parents' house?"

"Destroying evidence?" I suggest.

The back door opens, and Steve steps out onto the wooden deck. He's in a white button-up and khakis and wearing a ridiculous pair of aviator glasses that do not make him look like a young Tom Cruise, I don't care what his latest booty call told him. The sight of his stupid face makes rage boil through my veins. He made a serious mistake in judgment today, one that could've killed Cassie.

Being behind bars might be too good for him.

I'm so busy fighting the urge to charge and toss *him* in

the trash can that I almost miss the sack of garbage swinging from his hand.

"Oh, shit," I mutter.

Now I'm the asshole who both didn't believe Cassie *and* put my raccoon on a collision course with douchebag danger.

Blake grabs my shoulder before I can move. "Wait. George has this."

Steve flips open the trash can lid. He swings the bag inside without looking down and slams it closed again. Then he grabs the handle on both the recycling and the larger can—inside which my raccoon is probably freaking the hell out—and drags them down his driveway.

He drags and drags, while my heart slams against my ribs like a wrecking ball because any second I expect George to leap from the can and blow our cover, and our chances of getting the evidence to put Steve away, all to hell.

But miraculously, the bin stays closed. All the way down the driveway until Steve arranges them neatly on the street. The dickweed waits another breath-stealing moment, stretching his arms over his head like he's just finished moving something a hell of a lot heavier than bins on wheels, and then ambles back into the house, using the front door this time.

"Damn, that was close," I hiss as Blake exhales audibly beside me.

Not four seconds after the front door closes with an audible *whump*, George bursts from the can bearing loot slung around his neck. It looks like some sort of bag, or maybe…

"Is that a fanny pack?" Blake asks as George hustles back our way, looking pleased with himself.

I'm proud of him for obediently playing fetch for one

of the first times in his life, but I can't help but be disappointed in his find. Of all the incriminating things he could have potentially grabbed, Steve's fanny pack isn't high on the list.

Embarrassing as hell, but not a criminal offense.

"We'll have to send him back," I whisper to Blake, even as I pinwheel an arm and smile at George, coaxing him back to the tree line. "Later. After Steve hopefully gets his ass to his parents' house."

"No we don't," Blake says, nudging my arm. "Not according to the Supreme Court ruling on California vs. Greenwood."

I frown his way. "When did you get a law degree?"

"I watch *Law and Order* reruns when I can't sleep," he says. "And according to California vs. Greenwood, law enforcement can search trash left at the curb without a warrant. It's outside the curtilage, you see."

"I have no idea what that is, but if you're sure…"

"I'm sure." Blake tugs his phone out of his back pocket as George reaches our hideout. "I'll call the sheriff, tell him to get his ass out here right now."

"He won't come." I scoop George up, scratching his neck in silent praise. "Not without probable cause, and he's determined not to find any. He and Steve are tight as ticks." I glance down, grimacing at the S.B. monogrammed on the outside of the leather fanny pack. "How douche-y can this asshole get? His initials on a fanny pack? Jesus…"

George clacks in agreement, slapping my hand away as soon as I get the zipper open, and diving a paw into the bowels of his new treasure. The sound of delight he makes as he pulls out a flip phone is echoed by Blake's soft, "Oh, hell yes. A burner phone! Now we're talkin'."

"Let me see that, buddy," I say, tugging a little harder

when George resists. "I promise I'll give it back." With a cranky gurgle and a narrow-eyed glare that makes it clear he intends to keep an eye on me, George releases the cell. I hand it over to Blake, the man without an armful of raccoon.

"It's still charged enough to turn on," he says, excitement simmering in his voice. "Come on, baby, let's see what you've got. Okay, we've got the home screen, and now to see who Steve was secretly calling on his burner…" He taps two buttons before his hand goes still and a giant smile spreads across his face.

"Something suspicious?" I ask.

Blake turns the screen to face me, revealing a familiar number. "Only if you'd call ringing Cassie at five o'clock this morning, right when she got that creepy call from the guy trying to frame her suspicious."

It's all I can do not to let out a victory whoop. I do, however, high-five Blake twice and give George a gratitude-fueled belly scratch that leaves him humming blissfully in my arms.

"I'll call the sheriff's office and wait here to make sure he actually does a thorough search of whatever else is in those bins," Blake says, clapping me on the shoulder before guiding the fanny pack off George's neck. "You head back into town. You need to see a girl about an apology."

"I do," I agree. But this can't just be any apology. I need to do something special, something to show Cassie just how much she means to me.

Thoughts spinning, I head through the woods with George in my arms, swearing on everything he holds sacred that I will buy him a fanny pack and phone of his very own as soon as I make things right with Cassie.

As if he understands, somehow, he quiets down,

nodding in sober approval as I tug my cell from my pocket and make an InstaChat post. It's short and sweet, but it makes my point. At least I hope it does.

I don't know if Cassie will forgive me. I don't know if *I* can forgive me.

But I'm not giving up. And I hope Cassie will see that even when I'm an idiot, she's not alone.

That she's loved.

That she's wanted.

And that she has a home.

THIRTY-ONE

Cassie

I SPOT the sheriff crossing the square toward the bakery shortly before noon. My belly's full of delicious carbs—Savannah's right, this is totally the way to combat heartbreak—and my throat and lungs are less scratchy now, thanks to Gerald's honey tea.

"He's not taking you anywhere, hon," Ruthie May assures me.

"Not without going through me first," Gerald agrees.

I haven't called Savannah, and I'm not going to until I absolutely *have* to. Which is apparently going to be sooner rather than later.

"Maybe he's coming to tell me Steve gave him a full confession, and he's sorry," I say, but I don't believe it.

"Don't say a single word," Savannah's lawyer, Deborah, advises. "*Anything* you say in this town will get taken the wrong way."

"That's not true," Ruthie May objects.

Deborah clicks her manicured fingertips against the table and arches a thin blond brow.

"Okay, that's possibly true," Ruthie May concedes. "But we assume the best misinterpretation almost as often as we assume the worst. Look at all those people who didn't believe Steve would screw a sheep."

"And therefore assumed Savannah was making the entire thing up?" I remind her.

She pulls a face. "Bad example."

The sheriff reaches the door, then frowns and tilts his head toward the radio clipped to his uniform shirt. His voice—but not his exact words—carries through the glass door, and there's a muffled squawk back on his radio.

He pushes into the bakery and points at me. "You. Stay put."

And then he turns and hustles back the way he came.

"That was...unusual," Maud says.

"Maybe he got a call that his hemorrhoids are infected," Ruthie May says.

We all look at her.

She smiles sweetly. "What? That's not a good twist on a bad situation?"

I shove up from the table. "I have to use the ladies' room."

"If you're sneaking out the window, let me know. I'll meet you in the alley with the getaway car," Ruthie May offers.

"I'm not *running away*."

Her sweet smile widens. "I'm just assuming that if you were, you'd trust me to be your sidekick."

I fight a smile as I head to the bathroom. It *is* nice to have friends with their hearts in the right place.

Even if they can't erase everything that's gone wrong between Ryan and me.

When I get back to the table, Ruthie May and Maud are pressed to the window. "What on earth is that boy doing now?" Maud murmurs.

Gerald peers over their heads. "Can't be good if he's bringing the raccoon into it."

My heart stutters and my belly flips like I'm careening over the first big hill on a roller coaster.

I'm going to miss George.

"And what's the clothesline for?" Ruthie May says. "Why's he flapping his arms like that?"

"Where are all those people coming from?" Deborah the attorney asks.

Gerald starts to grin. "Cassie, hon...I think you need to see this."

I shake my head. I don't want to see.

Because if I see, I'll start to hope, and if I start to hope, I'll get crushed all over again.

"Come, come." Ruthie May dashes to my side and grabs one arm.

Maud takes the other.

"What—" I start.

"We're assuming the best about people," Ruthie May announces.

They pull me out the door to look at the square, which is slowly filling with people. Most of them are coming from the direction of the factory, but they're also coming from other directions too.

Ryan's in the center of the square, which he's divided with a clothesline. Even though he's half a city block away, the determination in the set of his jaw when our gazes lock makes the breath rush out of my lungs.

"I have an announcement," he calls. His voice carries, and the murmurs of the growing crowd settle down.

"Oh! He put it on InstaChat," Ruthie May whispers. *"Everyone come to the Square. I have a big fucking announcement."*

"*Shh!*" Maud hisses.

"Cassandra Mae Sunderwell did *not* sabotage Sunshine Toys. I know that for a fact, and so should all of you," Ryan announces.

There's a murmur in the crowd.

"I'm standing here, on this side of the line, because I'm on Team Cassie. I believe in her. The sheriff doesn't, but he's wrong. And any of you who don't believe her are wrong too."

My hand flies to my throat, tugging at the neck of the tee shirt dress I threw on after I was released from the hospital. What the hell is he doing?

"I don't care what you think of Sunshine Toys," he continues, "if you're not willing to stand up for one of our own when she's being framed, then you're not my friend or neighbor. So you can join me on Team Cassie, or you can be on the wrong side of history. Which is it going to be?"

"Is this really happening?" I whisper.

"I'll be damned," Gerald says while the people of Happy Cat all look at each other uncertainly.

Ruthie May's about to tremble herself out of her shoes from the excitement. "He's taking a stand," she whispers.

"For you," Maud adds. "You know what people love about Ryan? He never takes sides. He's the guy who lives and let lives, who tries to make *everyone* happy."

I blink.

"Who's with me?" Ryan demands. "Who's on Team Cassie?"

"I am," Blake announces, stepping up beside him.

"Me too." Jace joins Ryan as well.

"Me! Me!" Ruthie May dashes across the square, followed by Maud.

Gerald squeezes my shoulder, says, "I'll never be Team Sex Toy Factory, but I'm Team Cassie," and trails after his wife.

The teenagers who invented dildo ball trip over each other racing to Ryan's side, and are soon joined by Olivia. Then Emma June and Tucker.

Then Savannah's neighbors across the street.

Neil from the lab at the factory.

The farmer I accidentally christened with my chunk of sno-cone.

The couple who own the Kennedy Family Day School where I get my very favoritest coffee in the whole wide world.

"I've made a lot of mistakes," Ryan announces. His voice is steady, carrying across the square. "I'll probably make a lot more. But I will *never* doubt Cassie again. She's smart. She's kind. She has the purest heart of anyone I've ever known, and even if she *had* burned that factory down —WHICH SHE DID NOT— she would've had a damn good reason for it. And any of you who don't believe in her are no longer welcome at the annual O'Dell Halloween party."

There's a collective gasp, and at least fifty people rush toward the half of the square declared to be *Team Cassie*.

I swallow the lump forming in my throat, but I can't stop the hot prick of tears stinging my eyes.

He's staking his entire reputation on *me*.

Gordon the taxidermist strides across the square and ducks under the clothesline to join Ryan's side. So does Carl, the crankiest old man in town twelve years running.

Some of the Sunshine Toys employees who haven't been coming to work because they didn't want to be photographed by the building march up to his side.

"You don't have to like the factory to like Cassie," Ryan says. "I don't like Tucker's loud-ass motorcycle, but I still like him. I don't like Carl's snappy beagle or the catfish at the place my parents made me go to every Sunday as a kid or how everyone in this town lives to be in everyone else's business." He pauses, his voice gentling. "But we're neighbors. We're friends, family. Or at least I thought we were. But if we, as a community, can't embrace a woman as good as Cassie, then I don't think I can be a part of it anymore."

The Team Cassie half of the square is so full people are stretching the clothesline to fit onto that side.

I swipe my eyes, feeling both silly and overwhelmed.

Fool me once, I keep reminding myself as Ryan weaves through the crowd toward me. *Fool me once...*

Except I understand.

Ryan's a protector, he always has been. He looks out for the people he loves, and the drama and danger at the factory have been a threat to the things he holds most dear.

And this is his home.

It's been his home his entire life.

But he's still willing to give it all up—home, family, his standing in the community. For me. For a second chance.

And you believe in second chances, girl, my inner voice whispers as he stops on the sidewalk before me. She may have gotten a little smarter since I first came to town.

"Cassie," he says, my name a prayer on his lips. "I can say I'm sorry until the cows come home, and it still wouldn't be enough to tell you how much I regret the way I acted this morning."

I tuck my arms around myself and blink against fresh tears, looking over his head at the people in the square. Someone's pulled up "We Are Family" on their phone, and other people are holding up lighter apps and swaying to the music.

This town is so...perfect.

Funny and complicated and, yes, awful sometimes, but also...*perfect*.

"Team Cassie!" Tucker hollers.

"Shush up so we can hear him, doofus," Emma June hisses.

Ryan ducks his head and runs a hand over his mussed hair. He looks like he hasn't slept in days. Apparently being estranged from each other for the morning has been as hard on him as it's been on me.

"It's okay if you hate me forever," he says, "but I wanted to make sure you know you're not alone. You *fit* here, Cassie. I know how much the factory means to you. How much you want to do with it. You should stay. Shine. Embrace *all* of Happy Cat, the good and the bad, but know that these people—" He hooks a thumb behind him at the crowd, which is starting to sing along. "They have your back. And if you don't want anything to do with me, I'll leave. If that's what you need to be happy, I'll go."

"*No!*" I couldn't stop the strangled cry if I tried. It wells up from the depths of my heart and bursts out of me. I wipe at the stupid tears again. "No," I say again, softer. "You don't have to go. This is your home."

"And yours?" he asks.

The pain, uncertainty, and regret in his beautiful eyes are killing me. I want to wrap my arms around him and promise him everything's going to be okay, but I'm so scared.

Falling in love was the easy part. Fighting for love is harder than I ever imagined it could be. Because this fight isn't about putting up my fists, it's about letting down my walls and being vulnerable with this man who means so much to me. A man I now know without a doubt holds my heart in his hands.

He could break me. So easily.

Be he also makes me whole.

"George would miss you," he adds.

My laugh comes out half-sob. "That was low."

His lips hitch halfway up. "I'm a desperate man. I fucked it up with you. I know that. And I'm so sorry."

I sniff. "Yeah. You did fuck up. Why did you do that?"

He sighs, but he doesn't flinch in the face of my searching look. "I got a peek at what it might be like to lose you, and it scared the hell out of me. Shook me so hard I didn't realize I was running scared until my brothers knocked some sense into me." He swallows hard. "When I'm with you, everything feels so *right*, Cass. Like, for the first time in my life, I'm exactly where I'm supposed to be, doing exactly what I'm supposed to do. And that's loving you, with everything in me."

I press a fist to my chest, where my heart is threatening to pound a hole through my ribs.

"I'm not perfect," he continues, his eyes shining, "and I can't promise I won't fuck up again, but if there's any chance you could give me a second chance, I swear to you, I will bust my ass to be the man you deserve. If you want me to print my apology on the front page of the paper, I will."

My lips quirk. "I think the whole town's already heard it."

He huffs, blinking as he nods. "Yeah. You're probably

right. But…anything else. Anything at all. You name it, baby, and I'll do it. I just—I want to take back everything that happened this morning. I want to have never left our bed. I want to have been there for you when you needed me. Because you're what matters most. And I'm just so damned sorry."

I launch myself at him, because this isn't a man who wants to hurt me.

This is *my* man.

Who's as imperfect as I am, but who tries his best to be everything and more for the people he loves.

"Stop," I say, wrapping him up tight in my arms. "Stop apologizing. I forgive you. And I love you. Just the way you are."

He exhales a shaky breath and squeezes, his nose buried in my hair. "I love you, Cassie. I love you so much it hurts."

"It's not supposed to hurt," I tell him.

"Hurting you hurts me."

"I forgive you," I whisper again. "And I'm sorry for not forgiving you sooner. But even when I was mad at you, I still loved you. I've always loved you, Romeo."

"Ditto, Juliet."

Cheers are erupting behind us, but I shut them out and hug Ryan with all my might.

He's so much for so many people, but who takes care of *him*? I think that needs to be my job. And I think I'm going to kick ass at it.

He smiles at me with shiny eyes full of hope. "I don't know what I ever did to deserve you."

"You're *you*. That's more than enough."

A furry beast circles my legs and chitters at me. I look down at George, and he smiles back up at me.

Ryan brushes a thumb down my cheek. "Can I take you home?"

"In a minute."

His brows furrow. "If you're waiting for the sheriff, it's safe to say he has his hands full with the *real* criminal now."

A relief I didn't know I needed sags through my body. Having the entire town on my side is one thing. Convincing law enforcement is also necessary to staying out of jail, however. "Really?"

Ryan grins at me. "George caught himself an arsonist."

"Good boy," I tell George. "I'm making you extra popcorn tonight, and I want you to tell me all about it."

George doesn't clap his hands, but his beady expression tells me he's looking forward to being back where we belong. With popcorn. And Ryan. And each other, just like a real family.

"So, about home," Ryan says, taking my hands in his.

I shake my head again. "Nope. This first."

And before he can object—not that he would, I'm quite certain—I give the crowd what they want. I go up on tiptoe to press a kiss to his lips.

The quick kiss turns into a long kiss, and soon I've completely forgotten we're in public.

George hasn't, though.

He climbs Ryan like a tree, wedging his fluffy butt between us before any clothes are in danger of falling off.

We break apart, laughing. "Okay, okay," Ryan says to George. "We'll get a room."

All of Happy Cat explodes in cheers behind us, and I realize I've found something I'll never have in San Francisco.

I don't just have a true love, I have the love of a whole community.

But Ryan is my favorite. My very, very favorite.

That's true even before the photos of Steve being led into the sheriff's office in handcuffs break on InstaChat a few hours later. But when I hear how my man and my trash panda saved the day, I have no doubt I'm the luckiest woman in Georgia.

"You guys," I say, giggling as the comments and sheep emojis pile up on the InstaChat post. "You did so good."

Ryan kisses my temple, drawing me closer on the bed. As close as two people with a giant raccoon in their laps can get, anyway. But George insists on holding the tablet, even though he hasn't yet figured out how to work the screen. But with this brilliant little critter, I'm sure it's just a matter of time.

"We would've done anything for you," Ryan tells me. "We'll *always* do anything for you."

I lift a brow at him. "*Anything?*"

"Anything."

"Even put matching handlebars on your bike?"

He tips his head back and laughs, and I soak in the music of my favorite sound in the entire world.

"For you? Absolutely." He kisses me again, and I smile against his lips.

Because there's nothing I wouldn't do for Ryan either.

And I can't wait to spend the rest of my life showing him.

THIRTY-TWO

Ryan
One Month Later…

KARAOKE NIGHT at the Wild Hog has been pre-empted tonight by something better: the party for the formal launch of Cassie's new gaming app for Sunshine Toys.

Jace announced the party on InstaChat last week, and the event got so many RSVPs that he had to issue tickets. Since Steve ended up behind bars for a laundry list of offenses, including multiple counts of arson, Cassie's been pretty popular around here.

And the factory is gaining popularity too, at least to a degree.

Now, as I wade through the crowd with two lemonades in hand, looking for Cassie, it's all good vibes. Friends and neighbors shout greetings and congratulations, as if I'm the one who's done something special, when really, it's all my girl.

She came up with the plan to save Savannah's factory.

She charmed half the people who are still opposed to the factory into putting up with it just to keep her sweet self around.

And she's made me feel like a new man.

Until she came home, I had no idea what I was missing. No idea this kind of love was even possible. I don't know what I'll do if she ever changes her mind and decides to head back to San Francisco.

Other than follow her.

We haven't talked again about her work situation, but I know she can't work remotely forever. And she's been conducting interviews for a general manager for the factory in Savannah's absence, since it appears her sister isn't coming back from the UK anytime soon. And while Cassie's much more comfortable now with the factory's products, her first love is still game design.

I finally locate her playing Ms. Pac-Man, which is where I should've looked in the first place. "Hey, you."

She tilts her cheek to take a kiss.

"Hold on...one more...and *got it*!" She pumps a fist in the air and spins to grab my face and pull me down for a long smacker on the lips. I lift the lemonades out of the way and smile into her kiss. She's in a tee shirt she designed specifically to promote the new Love Your Inner Sunshine app.

Hers is blue with the Sunshine logo hugging a cute brunette in glasses and a bouncy ponytail.

Mine's black.

Jace and Blake both went for gray, and Ruthie May's running around in a purple version.

Cassie's eyes are bright and happy when she lets me go. "I beat my own high score," she informs me.

"You're supposed to be getting ready to make a speech."

She wrinkles her nose. "You know there's a reason I hide behind a computer screen as often as possible."

"Yeah, and I also know you can do this. Here." I hand her one sweating mason jar. "Liquid courage."

"Is it the courage part or the lemonade part that makes this so delicious?"

"Both."

We clink jars and each take a healthy gulp. She wraps an arm around my waist and leans her head against my heart. "Did I tell you initial projections suggest we'll triple sales within a week?"

"That's amazing. *You're* amazing."

"Nah. I'm just a girl who wants the world to get more comfortable with orgasms through gaming."

"Cassie! *Cassie*! They're waiting on your speech, hon." Ruthie May swats at my arm. "Let go, Ryan. You can take her home tonight. The rest of us get her for a couple hours."

Her eyes are twinkling as she pulls Cassie away.

I follow along behind them, nodding to Gerald and Maud as I pass them at the end of the bar. "Good to see you here," I tell them.

"We wouldn't miss it for the world," Maud replies.

"Just being a good neighbor," Gerald grumbles.

He's also made a point of dropping off donuts or muffins once a week at the factory as they've been rebuilding the damaged section over this past month. I clap him on the shoulder. "You're the best kind of neighbor."

He blushes. Maud claps delightedly.

And I grab the bottle of champagne Jace hands over

the bar, trading in my lemonade for something more festive.

I'm still worried about him and this baby and Ginger, but I probably will be for the rest of my life. Just need to get used to it.

"Hi, is this on?" Cassie winces. "Oh, wow, I'm loud."

Chuckles echo around the room while Cassie tucks her hair behind her ear and pulls back from the microphone. She's left her locks down tonight, and I can't wait to run my fingers through them again tonight.

That happens to be one of my very favorite pastimes.

I rub at my chest, because this is *it*.

This is the last major project Cassie needed to finish for Sunshine Toys.

She's been working hellacious hours to keep up with both her job back in San Francisco and to take Sunshine six levels higher than what it was when she got here. I have no idea what comes next, but I know it's going to be big. For a wee thing, Cassie always goes big.

"I just wanted to say thank you," she says. "To all of you. I know the factory isn't the most popular thing in town, but the fact that you're the kind of people to rally around your friends and neighbors to pitch in, even when it's uncomfortable, is what makes Happy Cat so amazing."

Ruthie May whoops, and Olivia lifts a glass containing a green gloop that suggests she smuggled in an avocado wheatgrass smoothie.

But I'm pretty sure she could smuggle in a live cow and do kombucha shots off its back and Jace wouldn't say a word. He lets her get away with things I've never seen him tolerate from other people and there's definitely a weird vibe between those two.

Cassie leans into the microphone again. "In the

gaming world, we have big parties to launch new products, which is technically why we're here tonight. To celebrate the Love Your Inner Sunshine app. But mostly, I wanted an excuse to have a party with you guys, the people who've been like family since I got back to town."

She graces me with a warm smile that sends champagne bubbles rising in my heart. "And I have a confession," she adds.

The entire room perks up, and I hide a smile. Nothing like a good confession to get people's attention.

"When I first came home," she says, "I was uncomfortable with Sunshine's products too."

I straighten, my eyes going wide, because if the next step is talking about what we did with some of those products the other night—

"But I've come to realize that there's more to all this than just physical satisfaction. Savannah's dream was to help women become stronger, braver, and more confident, and I think that's beautiful. My wish for *all* of you is that you love yourselves—bravely and fiercely—imperfections and all. You deserve it."

I sag in relief while everyone around me *aawwww*s.

"I didn't expect to be here learning so much about myself, or to be having so much fun, but for the first time in my life, I feel like I belong. And I love every last one of you so, so much."

"She's been drinking, hasn't she?" Ruthie May whispers.

"No, Ruthie May, I have *not* been drinking," Cassie answers. "But I have been thinking, and every day, it becomes more clear that I need to make a decision about my future. Because it turns out working remotely isn't something I enjoy much in the long term."

My heart stops. Right there in the Wild Hog.

But then she smiles in my direction, and it starts beating again.

"When Savannah and I were kids, this was home part-time. But it feels like a full-time home now. So, y'all are stuck with me." She stands up straighter, rolling her shoulders back. "So I want to take this opportunity to announce that I'm going into business for myself. If any Happy Cat business owners are looking for an app to draw in new customers or a snazzy new website, I'm your gal. I'm also going to start a coding class to get our kids ready to take on the world. Let's put this little town back on the map for *everything* we're good at as a community."

"Ooh, me!" Maud's hand flies into the air. "We want help at the bakery, Cassie! Dough on the Square first!"

"Get in line, Maud," Blake calls. "My winery is opening next year. Family first."

"I'm just as much family as you are!"

"Only if Cassie's living at your brother's house too."

Everyone laughs. I head to the stage, because this announcement definitely calls for champagne.

"Since you know where to find me," Cassie says with a shameless shrug and a smile tossed in my direction, "let's keep this party going! Thank you!"

She puts the mic back and steps right into my arms.

"That was the best speech I've ever heard," I tell her.

She laughs. "It was emotional love vomit."

"And it was beautiful. Just like you."

Blake jostles into us before I can kiss her. "Gimme that bottle. We're popping the top and celebrating." He winks at Cassie. "I knew you'd stay. Nice that you're making it official."

"I *do* still have to go back to San Francisco to clean out my apartment," she says, "but I'll be coming right back." She looks up to me. "You want to come with? We can take a few days, and I'll show you around. Give you a taste of the big city?"

I don't answer.

Not with words.

I'm too busy kissing the woman I'm going to love for the rest of my life.

EPILOGUE

Cassie

MY FEET ARE tired and I'm squeezed between too many people on the pier, but my heart is full and the late afternoon breeze is cooling my slight sunburn. We've had a long day playing tourist, and I feel like I've been introduced to a new side of the city I called home for so many years.

I loved seeing it through Ryan's eyes.

I nudge him and point to one of the sea lions. "Look! He's trying to push his friend off!"

We both laugh as the giant animals flap their fins and bark at each other on the docks. Six other sea lions sleep on, ignoring the commotion while another tries to get up on the wood shelf to sun himself.

Ryan tugs me closer with the arm around my waist, pressing a kiss to my hair. "The Golden Gate Bridge, the sourdough bakery, the Ghirardelli chocolate factory, and the sea lions. Today's been incredible."

"It's not over yet, mister. We still have a baseball game. And wine country tomorrow."

"Can't get this back in Happy Cat. You sure you want to leave?"

"Yep," I say, without a speck of doubt. "We can always come back to visit. But Happy Cat's home. You belong there. *We* belong there."

He bends down and captures my lips in a sweet kiss. "I love you, Cassandra Mae Sunderwell."

I cup his stubble-rough face and smile, my cheeks stretched so wide they hurt. "I love you too, Ryan O'Dell."

The sea lions all start barking, and we both laugh again. They're as bad as George, interrupting us when we get too close. Though in George's case, it's because he just wants in on the love too.

Olivia might be right.

Maybe he needs a special lady of his own. Maybe then, he'd quit scratching at the door when Ryan and I are having private time.

Speaking of private time…

I tilt my head back toward The Embarcadero, the main drag beside the piers. "You know, we have about two hours before the game starts, and our hotel is right there…"

That's generally all it takes to get Ryan hustling in the direction of home. Or a hotel room. Or anywhere we can find thirty minutes of privacy, really.

But he doesn't move.

Instead, his eyes turn serious as he studies me.

"Do I have chocolate on my cheek?" I start to swipe

at my face, but he captures my hand and shakes his head with a smile.

"No, you're just—you're absolutely perfect."

Heat flushes my cheeks warmer. "I'm not perfect, but you make me feel like I get pretty close."

"Then I'm doing something right."

"You do *everything* right."

He opens his mouth again, but pauses, his gaze searching mine again.

"What is it?" I ask softly.

"I just—it's barely been two months, but I can't remember a time when you weren't a part of me."

My already happy heart takes flight and bursts into song. "I know exactly what you mean. Like I found the missing piece I didn't know I was looking for."

"I worried this was too soon, but..." He trails off, taking my hands in his. And then he drops to his knee, making my jaw drop with a soft gasp. "Cassie, I always wanted to see the world. But when I'm with you, you're all the world I need. I want to spend the rest of my life making you as happy as you make me. Will you marry me?"

I launch myself at him, shouting, "Yes! *Yes*!" almost before he's finished. He catches me easily, and he kisses me, right there on our knees on Pier 39, with other tourists around us clapping and the sea lions barking out a celebration in the background.

"I don't have a ring yet—" Ryan starts.

I shake my head. "I don't need a ring. I just need *you*."

"You have me, Cassie. Always and forever. Hook, line, and sinker."

This man.

He's given me a home. He's helped me own my sexuality, love myself in a way I never did before, and have the courage to reach for my dreams with both hands. And now he's giving me happily ever after.

I laugh as I wrap him in a tight hug. "We're going to have the best life *ever*."

"So long as we're together," he agrees.

I stand, pulling him to his feet with me. "*Now* can we go see about those two hours in our hotel room?" I whisper with a wink.

"Anything my woman wants," he replies.

And just like the night he made love to me for the first time, he scoops me into his arms and carries me off into our bright, shiny future.

SNEAK PEEK FROM LILI VALENTE

AVAILABLE NOW FROM LILI VALENTE
The NHL's hottest bad boy is about to fall for his best friend's little sister…
Hot as Puck is out now.

Justin

This is it, the night I'll look back on in fifty or sixty years and stab a finger at as the moment my life changed forever. Somewhere out there, in the throng of people wiggling to the club beat pulsing across the Portland skyline from the most exclusive rooftop lounge in the city, is the woman I'm going to marry.

Next summer.

In eight short months.

Because I'm dying to settle down, develop a food-baby where my six-pack used to be, spend Friday nights on the couch in my give-up-on-life sweatpants arguing about what to watch on Netflix and picking out names for the five or six kids my wife and I will bang out as quickly as possible to ensure we'll have an army of small people to share in the grinding monotony of our wedded bliss.

Ha. Right.

Or rather *no*. Hell no. Fuck no, with a side of "what kind of reality-altering drugs have you been huffing in the bathroom?"

Sylvia is out of her goddamned mind! I'm twenty-eight years old—tonight, happy fucking birthday to me—and at the top of my game. I have zero interest in a long-term commitment to anything but my team.

The Portland Badgers are riding a ten-game winning streak, thanks largely to the fact that I bust my ass in the gym every other morning so I can bust my ass on the ice every time Nowicki spaces-out eighteen minutes into the period and forgets what his stick is for. That rookie's untreated ADHD is a pain in my ass, but the rest of the forwards and I are taking up the slack and then some. I'm averaging over a point a game, leading the league in goals, and on my way to an elite season. Maybe even an Art Ross Trophy-winning season, though I don't like to count my eggs before they've been scrambled, smothered in cheese and hot sauce, and wrapped in a burrito.

God, a burrito sounds good. I'm so fucking hungry. I would kill for Mexican right now, or at least something cooked and wrapped in something other than seaweed.

Nearly three thousand dollars in hor d'oeuvres are being passed around this party on shiny silver platters, and there's not a damned thing I want to eat.

I let Sylvia—who has very firm opinions about many, many things—handle ordering the food, and apparently she thought sushi, sushi, more sushi, and some weird, rock-hard, low-fat cookies that taste like vanilla-flavored air were all anyone would want to shove in their pie-hole tonight. Just like she thought I should get down on one knee and put a ring on her finger in time to plan a blockbuster summer wedding or she would need to "explore her other options."

Explore her other fucking options. What the fuck? Who says something like that to a guy they swear they're desperately in love with? If she were really that gone on me, wouldn't I be the *only* option? The only person in the entire world that she could even remotely consider spending the rest of her life with?

I kind of want to hate Sylvia—what sort of person tries to blackmail you into proposing to them on *your* birthday? She should have at least waited until *her* birthday next month—but I just keep thinking about how lonely my bed is going to be tonight. Sylvia is clearly deeply deluded about how far along we are in the evolution of our relationship, but she's also very pretty, gives the best head I've ever had, bar none, and smells really, really nice.

I have a thing about the way a woman smells. Not her perfume or her soap or her body lotion, but *her*. The woman herself. Her base note, the scent that rises from her skin when she's lying in the sun or kissing me after a run or just hasn't showered in a while.

Yes, with the right woman, I enjoy logging some quality bedroom time while she's a little bit dirty. Don't fucking judge me! It's my birthday!

Anyway... No one smells as good as Sylvia does at the end of a long day on my boat, with sweat, sea salt, and sunscreen dried on her skin. Making love to her on the deck this past summer, with her long legs wrapped around my waist as I did my best to take home the trophy for most orgasms delivered in a single afternoon, I was convinced I'd finally met someone I could stick with for longer than a season.

But it's not going to happen. It's only October and I've just told Sylvia she's coo-coo for Cocoa Puffs and that I'll have her shit packed up and sent to her office tomorrow afternoon.

And then she said that I was an emotionally unavailable jerk who is incapable of sustaining an adult relationship. And then I said that she's a blackmailing, birthday-ruining, manipulative, sushi-obsessed control freak who should try to choke down a carb once in a while because it might make her more fun to be around on pizza night or donut morning or any other day of the goddamned week involving carbs because a life without carbs is a stupid life. And then she flipped me off and told me to "have a nice long, lonely existence, asshole," before knocking over a tray of champagne glasses on her way to the elevator at the other end of the roof.

The only good news? Very few of my guests seemed to notice our fight or Sylvia's dramatic exit.

It's nine-thirty, we've all been drinking since six, and most of my nearest and dearest are feeling no pain. I should be feeling no pain, too. I'm on my third tumbler of GlenDronach, haven't eaten anything since lunch because the food at my party is unacceptable—if Sylvia and I were really meant to be, she would have realized I hated sushi two months ago—and haven't drunk anything more serious than a beer since before the preseason.

But somehow, I'm stone-cold sober.

Sober and tired of celebrating, and wishing I could slip out and grab a deep-dish pizza from Dove Vivi. The cornmeal crust thing they've done to their pies is addictive, and I'm pretty sure there's nothing in the world fresh mozzarella, house-made bacon, and a hearty slathering of pesto can't fix.

Portland is home to some of the best eats in the world.

It's also home to more strip clubs per capita than any other city in the nation. If I weren't committed to being a good host, I could have pizza in my belly and boobs in my face in under an hour. But I'm not the kind to ghost on my guests. I leave that for weirdos like my team captain, Brendan, who consistently vanishes from bars and clubs without warning, and clearly has issues with saying good-bye.

Not that I can blame him. After six years as a happily married man, going back to hitting the scene solo can't be easy.

I'm just glad to see him finally out and about again. After Maryanne's death, he shut down so hard a lot of us on the team were worried there might come a day when we'd show up for practice and learn Brendan wasn't coming back to the ice, either because he'd lost the will to play, or because he'd lost the will to live.

That's how much you should love the woman you're going to marry. You should love her so much that if she were taken away from you it would feel like your rib cage had been cracked open and some sadistic son of a bitch was cutting away tiny pieces of your heart, slathering them in salt, and eating them right in front of you.

I've never felt anything close to that. For Sylvia or any other girl I've dated.

So maybe Sylvia is right. Maybe I'm going to spend the rest of my life solo, with my loneliness occasionally broken by short-term relationships with various hot pieces of ass.

"Poor me," I say, lips curving in a hard grin.

Seriously, cry me a river, right? I've got a multi-million-dollar contract, a stunning loft with one-hundred and eighty degree views of the city, and my health, which is not something I'm stupid enough to take for granted. I was born with the kind of face that not even a black eye from scrumming with those douchebags from L.A. can wreck, and a body that performs—on the ice and in the bedroom. I should be laughing all the way to the dance floor, where I know of at least six or seven unattached hotties, any one of which would be happy to ease my birthday breakup pain by riding my cock all night long.

What do I want instead?

Pizza. My pajamas. And a crochet hook with an endless supply of yarn.

Nothing calms me down like hooking on a granny square until I've got one big enough to cover my entire damned bed. I've graduated to more complex projects since those early days learning how to hook so I wouldn't go crazy while I was stuck in bed with mono for three months, but sometimes mindless repetition is the only cure for what ails me.

And yes, I like to crochet. Again, I'll ask that you not fucking judge me, because it's my birthday, because my charity, Hookers for the Homeless, has provided over two thousand caps, gloves, and scarves to people in need, and because my Instagram account—Hockey Hooker—has over a million followers. Clearly, the women of the world have no problem with a man who enjoys handicrafts. Though, the fact that my first post was a body shot of me wearing nothing but a Santa Hat I'd crocheted over my cock probably didn't hurt.

I have no shame when it comes to selfies with my latest project. My friend Laura—childhood partner in crime and current public relations master for the Badgers—says she approves of my social media efforts to promote good will for the team. Her little sister and my crochet guru, Libby, thinks it's great that I'm using my yarn addiction to raise awareness of the homeless crisis. But let's get real. I started posing semi-nude for the tail and the attention.

I'm usually a big fan of tail and attention.

But now, as Laura and Libby climb the steps leading up to the patio from the dance floor, clearly intending to wish me a warm, bubbly, old-friends happy birthday, I wish I had an excuse not to talk to either one of them. Laura because she's insane when she's drunk—once she's had a few, the usually level-headed La can't be trusted not to embarrass herself and everyone around her—and Libs because I'm incapable of hiding anything from that girl.

Ever since thirteen year old Libs spent months teaching me how to crochet when I was housebound my sophomore year of high school—keeping me company and furthering my yarn-based education while we watched 80s movies and debated important things like whether *Better Off Dead* or *Just One of the Guys* was the superior underrated teen flick of that particular decade—I've had a chink in my armor where the youngest Collins sibling is concerned.

She sees through me. Every damned time.

When I had a shitty first half of my first season with the Badgers five years ago, Libby was the one who noticed I was being eaten alive by self-doubt and talked me back from the edge. When my charity was getting audited by the IRS, Libby realized I wasn't nearly as chill about the whole thing as I was pretending to be and sent me a knight's helmet she'd crocheted and a note promising that everything would work out. And when Sylvia and I had a pregnancy scare last summer, Libby was the only person I told.

Hearing Libs say that I could absolutely handle being a dad had made me a little less terrified. Not that I'd believed her, but hearing that trying your best and loving your kid is all that really matters from a woman who spends every day with a classroom full of rug-rats was comforting.

But I don't want to be comforted right now. I want to get through the rest of this party and then hide out at home and lick my breakup wounds in private. So I plaster on a smile and hope it's too dark for Libby to see how shitty I feel.

"Hello, birthday boy!" Laura throws her long arms around me, hugging me hard enough to make my breath rush out with an *oof* as she crushes my ribs, reminding me she's also freakishly strong when she's three sheets to the wind. "I love you, Justin. I'm so glad we're still best friends. Let's go do happy-birthday shots on the roof to celebrate!"

"We're already on the roof." I grunt again as she hugs me even tighter.

"Yes, we are, and as high up as anyone needs to be right now," Libby agrees, meeting my pained gaze over her sister's shoulder, her brown eyes anxious. Clearly, she's also aware that her big sis has entered the bad-decision-making portion of the evening and should be monitored closely until she's home in bed.

"No, the real roof, the one through the locked door behind the DJ booth." Laura points a wobbly hand toward the stairwell on the other side of the dance floor, then twists her long red hair into a knot on top of her head. "I've been practicing my lock-picking skills so I'll be ready when I quit PR to become a spy."

"As one does," I observe dryly.

"Exactly!" Laura jabs a bony finger into the center of my chest. "See, you get it. So let's do this. We'll break the lock, climb the stairs, and be the highest things in downtown. Get shots and meet me there. Or maybe we should stick with martinis." She moans happily as she wiggles her fingers in the general direction of the bar. "Those Thai basil martinis are so amazing! Perfect with the sushi. Like, seriously brilliant. Sylvia did a bang-up job with the catering, Jus. Especially for a woman who looks like she hasn't eaten since last Christmas."

"Laura, hush," Libby whispers, nudging her sister in the ribs with her elbow.

Laura bares her teeth in an "oh shit" grimace before smacking herself on the forehead. "Fuck, I'm sorry. I forgot about the storming out and knocking over a tray of drinks on her way out of the party thing. Are you two okay?"

"We're fine," I say, cursing silently. So much for avoiding this particular conversation. "She just decided it wasn't working for her. It's no big deal."

"But breaking up on your birthday sucks." Laura's lips turn down hard at the edges. "And I thought she was one of the nice ones. I mean, I didn't know her that well, but she seemed nice."

"She was nice." I take another too big drink of my scotch. "And now she's gone. But she hadn't even unpacked her boxes yet, so it shouldn't take long to move them all out."

"That's right. I forgot you two had moved in together. Bet that makes you want to keep drinking, huh?" Laura reaches back, putting an arm around Libby, hugging her much shorter sister closer as she not-so-subtly tries to steal Libby's martini.

Libby, who I suddenly realize is looking very un-Libby-like in a tight black tank top and a pair of leather pants that cling to her curvy thighs, huffs and swats Laura's hand away. "Enough! Stop using displays of affection to try to steal my drink."

"Why? It worked last time," Laura says, grinning wickedly.

"Well, it's not going to work this time. I'm keeping my martini." Libby narrows her eyes, which are ringed in heavy black liner and some silver glittery stuff that emphasizes how enormous they are. It's a look that's way more rock-star than kindergarten teacher and also decidedly…odd. For her, anyway.

I can't remember the last time I saw Libby wearing makeup or tight clothing. She's a "layers of linen draped around her until she looks like an adorable bag lady or a hippie pirate" kind of girl. I'm used to the Libby who wears ruffly dresses, clogs, and crocheted sweaters, and totes her knitting bag with her everywhere she goes.

This new look is so unexpected that I'm distracted long enough for Laura to snatch my scotch right out of my hand.

"Hey, give that back," I say, scowling as she dances out of reach. "It's an open bar, psycho. Go get your own scotch."

"But it's more fun to steal yours," Laura says. And then, with the gleeful giggle of a woman who is going to be very hungover tomorrow morning, she turns and flees into the throng of dancers writhing to the music, tossing, "Come get me when it's time to break and enter! You know you want to," over her shoulder.

Libby sighs heavily, and I turn back to see her watching me with that same anxious expression, making my heart lurch. "I don't want to talk about Sylvia," I say, cutting her off before she can ask.

"Okay," she says, letting me off the hook far more easily than I expect her to. "But can we talk about something else? Something kind of…private?"

"Um, sure." I do a quick scan of our immediate

surroundings. Aside from a couple making out in the shadows about ten feet away, we're alone. Everyone else is either out on the dance floor, queued up at the bar, or lounging on the couches near the fire pit on the other side of the patio, soaking in the view of the city.

"Thanks." Libby smiles nervously as she lifts her glass. "Just let me down a little more liquid courage first."

"All right," I say, wondering who this woman is and what she's done with my sweet, rarely drinks more than one drink, doesn't own a stitch of black clothing, would never leave the house without putting on a bra Libby.

I really don't think she's wearing a bra under that lacy shirt. And I really can't stop staring, trying to solve the bra or no-bra mystery, and I'm swiftly becoming way too fixated on Libby's breasts for my personal comfort.

"Maybe I should get a drink, too." I start for the bar, needing a moment to pull myself together, when Libby puts a hand on my arm.

"I'm sorry," she says, but I have no idea what she's apologizing for, only that her touch feels different than it did before. As different as the Libby I've known since she was a kid is from this seriously sexy woman standing in front of me.

SNEAK PEEK FROM PIPPA GRANT

If you love hockey players and friends with benefits romance, read on for an excerpt of **Charming as Puck**...

Nick Murphy (aka a hockey god on the verge of being demoted back to mortal status)

Kami stayed over. That's weird. I must've drank too much last night. Or she did.

Actually, is she still drunk?

She doesn't usually lick my ear. Or sleep in my bed. We don't do breakfast together unless it's some godawful early morning meeting demanded by my sister, in which case we pretend we're just the same old friends who don't bump uglies, because Felicity would fucking kill me.

However, risk of death aside, if Kami's up for something this morning, I could get on board.

My dick's already showing off.

My eyes are still gritty. I definitely had too much to drink last night. I barely remember Kami showing up at all after the game last night. It was our season opener, at home, our first regular season game after winning the cup last year, and it was fucking brutal.

"Lower," I tell Kami, my voice ragged in my throat, angling my head, because being licked is nice, but if she's going to lick me, she could go for somewhere better than my ear.

"*Mmmoooooooo,*" she answers.

She licks my ear again, reaching the tip of her tongue right into my ear canal, and I lift a heavy arm to guide her face.

And then I freeze.

She's...furry.

Like a smooth kind of furry.

And I'm king of morning breath, but she smells worse than my sister after one of those vegan wheatgrass garlic avocado smoothies she likes to drink.

"Kami?" I rasp out.

"*Mmmooooooo.*"

I touch her face.

My eyes fly open.

Kami has blue eyes.

The eyes staring back at me are brown.

And huge.

And set behind a thick fuzzy brown snout, beneath a rigid brow line, with ears sticking up where I expected to see morning bed head.

"*Fuck!*"

I trip over the tangled sheets while I leap up, my head swimming. The cow watches me with those calm brown orbs. "*Mmmmooooooo,*" it says again in its baby cow voice.

Shit shit *shit*. "*Ssshhhh,*" I hiss at it.

I can't decide what to think first. My head's pounding. I'm going to fucking kill my brother-in-law, who is absolutely behind this, unless Kami's a shapeshifting cow, which isn't possible, even when I'm hung over.

Also, after the duck incident, if I get caught with another unapproved animal in my condo, I'm gonna get fucking kicked out of the building.

I don't have time to move. The season's just starting. My parents would move me, but I'm thirty fucking years old. *My parents aren't going to move me.*

Especially since if they did, they'd probably move me into their house, and that's not happening.

I might be playing in my home city, but I am *not* moving in with my parents.

I fumble in the dim light, looking for my phone. "Don't shit in my bed," I tell the cow. "I'll get you out of here, just please don't shit in my bed."

My phone's not where it belongs. It's not by my bed. It's not on my dresser. It's not in the bathroom.

My pants.

Maybe it's still in my pants.

Where are my—*fuck*.

My pants are under the cow.

It moos at me again. I fist my hair and stare at it. "Get up," I tell it.

It stares back.

It also doesn't move.

Or *mooooooo*ve, I can hear my teammates saying.

I grab one pant leg and pull. The cow sniffs at my dangling dick. I move out of the way, because I'm *not* into getting my family jewels licked by a freaking baby farm animal, even if said baby farm animal weighs three hundred pounds.

I'd wonder where the fuck Ares found a baby cow, except I, too, know a thing or two about delivering unexpected livestock to apartment buildings.

And the fucker just one-upped me.

For a quiet dude, he's fucking *evil*. He better never put a baby cow in Felicity's bed or he'll wake up strapped to the underside of an elephant halfway around the world.

I tug and pull on my pants, the cow gives an indignant baby *moo*, and *finally*, my jeans come free.

Without the phone in the pocket.

I press my palms into my eye sockets and think.

There was the game.

Vegas scored on me twice. We still won, because Ares and Frey and Lavoie were on fire, but I shouldn't have let Vegas score. Could've blocked both shots.

Skipping Chester Green's with the team afterwards. Opening a bottle of Jack at home. Texting Kami because I knew I shouldn't drink alone.

She showed up with that wide, borderline innocent smile. I was buzzed. She teased me about it. Said she wasn't going to take advantage of me.

Turned on *The Mighty Ducks*.

I fucking love that movie.

I talked her out of her pants before the Ducks won their first game, and—and that's where my phone is.

Next to the bottle of Jack I finished in the living room after Kami left.

The baby cow stares at me, those eyes bright and friendly and asking for love.

I trip into my jeans and head for the living room. The sun's telling me I need to get my ass in gear and over to the rink for morning skate before long. I snag my phone off the end table by my leather sofa, and I don't think twice as I dial a video call.

Kami's soft brown eyes come into focus, along with that wide smile. "Morning, sunshine. You feeling okay today?"

"How do I get a cow out of my bed?"

She wrinkles her brows at me. She's walking somewhere—the buildings behind her make me think she's heading to her office—and her brown hair's tied back in a ponytail that's whipping in the wind. "A cow out of your bed?" she repeats.

I flip the camera on my phone and march into my bedroom, watching the screen while I center my bed and the cow for her. "Yeah. A fucking baby cow in my fucking bed."

She nods thoughtfully. "Huh. That does appear to be a calf. Happy birthday to you too."

"It's not my fucking birthday. It's a fucking prank. Can you take care of it?"

Her expression goes still. "Can I...what?"

"Get it out of my condo. It's an animal. You're an animal doctor."

Silence.

Even her expression is silent, which is odd, because Kami's expressions are always big and loud and...and *expressive* and shit. Not because she's loud. She just *likes* things.

Like an optimist.

Yeah.

She's cheery. She makes loud, happy faces.

Fuck, I need to quit drinking.

"I *said*, *happy birthday to you too*," she says.

I squint at the phone. Since when does Kami talk in code? In the six months we've been banging behind my sister's back, the only code we've ever used is *I'm calling it an early night*. "Look, I know you probably think I deserve this after the donkey thing, but I have to get to morning skate, and we're flying out to Colorado after the game tonight, and I don't want to come home to a dead baby cow. I'll pay whatever it takes. But it—"

"Fine. Whatever. I'll take care of it."

I freeze.

I know that tone.

That's *pissed off woman* tone. And yeah, it's probably rude of me to call Kami first thing in the morning like this, but we're friends. I'd help her get a cow out of her place if I had time, but during the season, it's hockey first. Always.

"Thanks, Kami. I owe you—"

"Nothing, Nick. You owe me *nothing*. In fact, you can consider this a goodbye present. Because this little arrangement we have? It's over. I'm *done*."

She disconnects, and I'm left staring at my official team photo on the background of my phone.

I don't know what just happened, but I have a feeling it's worse than waking up with a baby cow.

ABOUT THE AUTHORS

Pippa Grant is a stay-at-home mom and housewife who loves to escape into sexy, funny stories way more than she likes perpetually cleaning toothpaste out of sinks and off toilet handles. When she's not reading, writing, sleeping, or trying to prepare her adorable demon spawn to be productive members of society, she's fantasizing about chocolate chip cookies.

Find Pippa at…
www.pippagrant.com
pippa@pippagrant.com

Author of over forty novels, *USA Today* Bestseller Lili Valente writes everything from steamy suspense to laugh-out-loud romantic comedies. A die-hard romantic and optimist at heart, she can't resist a story where love wins big. Because love should always win.

When she's not writing, Lili enjoys adventuring with her two sons, climbing on rocks, swimming too far from shore, and asking "why" an incorrigible number of times per day. A former yoga teacher, actor, and dancer, she is also very bendy and good at pretending innocence when caught investigating off-limits places.

You can currently find Lili in the mid-South, valiantly trying to resist the lure of all the places left to explore.

Find Lili at www.lilivalente.com

ALSO BY THE AUTHORS

Books by Pippa Grant
Mister McHottie (Chase & Ambrosia)
Stud in the Stacks (Parker & Knox)
The Pilot and the Puck-Up (Zeus and Joey)
Royally Pucked (Manning and Gracie)
Beauty and the Beefcake (Ares and Felicity)
Rockaway Bride (Willow and Dax)
Hot Heir (Viktor and Peach)
The Hero and the Hacktivist (Rhett and Eloise)
Charming as Puck (Nick and Kami)
Find more at Pippa's website, www.pippagrant.com

Books by Lili Valente
Hot as Puck
Sexy Motherpucker
Puck Aholic
Puck Me Baby
The Baby Maker
The Troublemaker
Magnificent Bastard
Spectacular Rascal
Dark Domination
and more!
Learn more at Lili's website, www.lilivalente.com.

Made in the USA
Monee, IL
03 March 2020